Also by Lydia Millet

Omnivores

George Bush, Dark Prince of Love

MY HAPPY LIFE

MY

HAPPY

LIFE

A NOVEL

Lydia Millet

Henry Holt and Company   •   New York

The author gratefully acknowledges the support of the Blue Mountain Center. She wishes to thank Maria Massie for her instincts and Elizabeth Stein for her conviction.

Henry Holt and Company, LLC
Publishers since 1866
115 West 18th Street
New York, New York 10011

Henry Holt® is a registered trademark of
Henry Holt and Company, LLC.

Library of Congress Cataloging-in-Publication Data
Millet, Lydia, 1968–
    My happy life : a novel / Lydia Millet.—1st ed.
        p. cm.
    ISBN 0-8050-6846-5 (hb)
        1. Psychiatric hospital patients—Fiction. 2. Mentally ill
women—Fiction. 3. Solitude—Fiction. I. Title.

PS3563.I42175 M9 2002
813'.54—dc21   2001039308

Henry Holt books are available for special promotions and
premiums. For details contact: Director, Special Markets.

First Edition 2002

Designed by Kelly S. Too

Printed in the United States of America
10   9   8   7   6   5   4   3   2   1

MY HAPPY LIFE

1

The door is locked from the outside; they went away and forgot me. It is not difficult: many times I have almost forgotten myself.

Because the world is full. It is teeming with us.

What happened was, the last one who remembered me was gone. It was Jim the night orderly, who faded away. And then the others left too. They closed the hospital and left me in this room, which was locked. And is still.

The swinging ball has not yet come. I think the building is waiting. Sometimes I think that I hear it sigh, like an old dog sleeping.

So now I seem to be alone. That is, if anyone saw me, they would take me for alone.

But I am not alone. I have you.

And aloneness is only a ghost. It likes to seep through cracks, at night or in the winter. But there are no cracks here. Here I feel sewn up, surrounded by substance like a nut in velvet or an eye in a sock. The room is seamless and all over my skin, enclosing. To keep me company, I have both dreams and memories.

Excuse me: if I could open the door I would leave, certainly. Or if the door melted, white steel turning to liquid, and flowed out between its own edges, bending like a spoon and spreading across the floor in a lake of metal, I would also walk out in that case. If the lake never cooled I would still walk, letting the soles of my feet turn into fire. Even if my legs began to melt, I would see just beyond the door before I fell. What lies there is the rest of everything. And the people I never knew and who never knew me.

How I miss them.

And also, I am always ready for an unexplained event: the melting of the door. I have heard myself promise many times that if I should wake up on the small, hard bed one morning and see the walls sliding and caving in, running thick as honey around my bedposts, I will not hesitate but stand and go.

As yet there have been no signs of melting.

But there are other ways to leave a room.

I have no matches, or maybe I could burn the walls. For light there are two bulbs in my ceiling, which have never yet given out. I keep them good by lighting the bedroom only while I write, and never lighting the bathroom. I have no television and no books and no food.

And of course no windows.

What I have is a shoebox, containing some other things: the stubs of several pencils I once was given, for example, and the dull blade of a razor, which I sharpen them with. I found the razor blade in the drain of my bathtub, slitting my longest finger as I grasped for it, glinting down there in the dark tunnel. It had caught on the crosshairs of the pipe.

I also have a threadbare towel, a small tooth, a flattened, pressed leaf from a tree named ginkgo, and one pale blue oval of glass within a silver rim, thin as the skin of an onion, by which I remember my happy life. And I have two paper shoes with elastic and ruffles around the ankles. These things are lovely.

On my person I bear other memories: one foot that is bent from the ankle and a design on my back like bending reeds, raised from the skin. I have an ear that is garbled and rippled into the shape of a frilly mushroom, where the cartilage has knitted itself into twists and flounces. I have purple spots that cover my kneecaps, bruises that are not fading, and an orange plastic hospital bracelet around my wrist that bears my date of admission. I cannot take it off. This bracelet is a survivor.

I once heard it said that rocks are majestic, rocks and mountains that hold themselves jagged and grand over the humble valleys. They are great because of their very long lives, and how beneath them many smaller things die. So if that which lives forever is best, my bracelet is like a god.

And some things are missing that should be with me, or not quite as they should be, and they too are memories I have gathered. Such as my hair, which all turned white long ago. So that now, though I am not yet ancient, to someone whose vision was only slightly blurred I would seem to be eighty.

But I am not eighty. I do not think I am forty, even. But excuse me, I am no longer sure. I have forgotten certain details, such as the year we are in.

Because a year of the world is not the same as a year of the body.

And there is the torn corner of a ten-dollar bill, a scrap of paper with words written on it, and a stiff brown pod, flattened like an umbrella on an old stem, from a vase of dried flowers. It has round holes in it that once held seeds.

These are not pleasing to me but I keep them anyway.

And often, to fall asleep, I think of a great white bird. It is bigger than an airplane; its wings are wide and strong. I think that I am lying nestled in the hollow between one of the wings and the gentle great back, and I feel the wings very slowly lifting and falling as the bird carries me.

Sometimes I get frightened suddenly that I will fall off, and then I have to imagine threads or ropes, impossibly soft but impossibly strong, that fasten me to the great bird loosely. If I tumble, they catch me and draw me back without shock.

And on the back of this great white bird with wise dark eyes and a noble long bill, I fly over the country. The feathers of the bird are downy and keep me warm and dry. And below us the mountains and the rivers and oceans stretch along endlessly. There is a green, rolling patchwork of farms.

And the wings beat beneath me.

I smooth the towel over my purple knees; I hold the deli-cate blue oval up to where the light comes from, on the ceiling. I am used to the dimness and I can see in it. The bulb above the bed lies in a convex disk of some nearly opaque matter, and if I stare for a long period of time I can see the bodies of moths and flies in the shallow basin. I will not eat them, not only because I cannot reach but also because I have never been able to eat what once moved itself on purpose.

I know the hospital has been abandoned by the deep silence beyond the walls. And the hot water stopped coming when the heat of the walls and air faded. At first, when the heat went, I tested the walls for faint sound. I beat on them with knuckles first and then the heels of my hands, asking if anyone heard me, in case there were some others. But either the walls are fortresses or I am the only one left here.

I drink cold water from the bathroom tap to fill my stomach, but I am getting thinner. There is a dent scraped in the plaster of the wall, from an occasion several days ago when I scratched at it with a pencil and tried to eat the powder. I would not advise this.

If there are others beyond the density of walls, likewise forgotten in dim rooms like this, I would caution them against it.

Long ago I finished the toothpaste, the shampoo, and the soap. They were not tasty either, although the toothpaste was by far the best. I had to tear the tube open and lick out the insides. How hard it was surprised me. I used one of my pencils to make the first puncture.

I miss the days and nights. Time is the same in here, and goes on. All I can do is hold each object carefully and think. So that the hours begin to move again. And I can write in small letters on the walls that cannot be eaten.

Box

Science has many laws, apparently. Of all of them I only know two: there is a force called gravity, and the universe came from a speck.

Myself I came from a box marked *Brown Ladies Narrow 8*, which had been left on a street. So I spent some of the first times I recall in a building not unlike how this one used to be: immense and patrolled by a legion of Mrs., who were often quite large and portly. One of the

Mrs., a Mrs. Ray, once told me she had found the box on a wet sidewalk in a long steady drizzle of rain.

During the night the rain had soaked the box. She came upon it in the morning, while she was carrying a bag of garbage to the curb with an umbrella in her other hand, and saw that it contained something naked, cold, blue, and slippery. At first she mistook it for an ugly doll, and then a dead body. Until my mouth opened and made a circle, like a fish after a hook. "You gaped like a fish," said Mrs. Ray. So this was how, said Mrs. Ray, I first became a beneficiary of the kindness of the state.

And this was also when I first became alone. I was quite fortunate since, if the habit of being alone is gained when people are still young, they will not mind it so much later.

She told me about the box's discovery, and when I asked her if they still had it anywhere she said that all the boxes were kept in the basement. I went down to the basement and sat among the shelves. They were piled high with boxes, so many that I then believed, for some years afterward, that each of the children had come in a box and had one of their own. I found my box at last, the one she had described. It was faded green, with markings on the end, and had the porous feel of cardboard that has been waterlogged before. Such cardboard molts at the touch of a finger, drops its frail skin in rolls and pills. It said *Brown Ladies Narrow 8*. And it was full of nails.

I turned it upside down and let the nails rain onto my lap; and I have carried it with me since then.

• • •

Now Mrs. Ray, who had the beauty of a horse or of a cow when she was eating, great, placid, square, and soft, and munching very slowly, was prone to tell me of the kind justice of the state most evenings and most days. She also liked to tell me of the kind justice of the church, and of policemen, and the Protective Services, and also of herself. She said, "We all have our crosses to bear. Oh mighty mighty oh."

This was between the foster families, when many of us came back to the buildings to wait. It was in the waiting place that we always came back to.

"You are extra," said Mrs. Ray, nodding and munching at the long table, one time when I had left a family with too many of us there. "Nobody needs you. It is overpopulation."

The family was the Rubens, and my favorite was thin Mr. Rubens with big teeth and an Adam's apple. Mr. Rubens put a bag on his head.

"Poor Mr. Rubens, mercy mercy me," said Mrs. Ray when I first told her how I saw Mr. Rubens—when the baby cried loudly—sitting, staring, and putting holes in his own knee with the knife that he usually used for the fish.

Mr. Rubens said to me, "Get me a plastic bag from under the sink."

Then he sprayed a can into the bag and tied it around his neck over his head. Flopping, he danced. With his face pinkly invisible. We could see his mouth stretched like an O between the letters of the pink writing on the bag, *A&P.*

When he fell down and we were all of us crying, I, being the oldest, called Children's Protective Services and said, "Mr. Rubens put a bag on his head."

Soon the apartment was teeming with kind policemen and kind paramedics. Mrs. Rubens chewed gum.

Anyway, when I asked why it happened, Mrs. Ray said, "Too many kids for the Rubens. She wanted the money, but he was a depressive and on medication. That is not allowed."

And then Mrs. Ray became quite agitated, as she was sometimes prone to be when she was under the influence. As she called it to me. She clenched her teeth and said, "The lying, lying bitch! She lied a blue streak. She lied enough to bring the maggots of Satan squirming from the ground."

I said, "Excuse me?"

That was what Mr. Rubens had taught me to say, in the event of confusion. He smiled often and counseled me: "Don't say what. Say excuse me or pardon me."

I thought he was a kind, kind man, yet kinder than the justice of the state, which was not yet apparent to me. He taught me a few things before placing the bag on his head. He taught me several ways in which to be polite. Including lifting a hand to your mouth when you cough. He liked to say, when he taught me something, "Do that for me. And I will not have lived in vain."

That was when Mrs. Ray said, "She wanted the extra money. Which the government pays for you, extra money for extra bodies."

I told Mrs. Ray about a memory I thought I had. In the dream I was in a place before I was born, the place that I came from. And there were crowds of people stretching to the horizon. They waited and they waited still. And then they were behind me, gone.

I felt sorry for them but certainly did not know why. And I knew that they also felt sorry for me. Some water was suspended in the air between us, water that carried sound and warmth. And in the vapor of the atmosphere all sorrows mingled in my eyes. Nothing stayed separate and so the sorrows made a tender bridge.

But Mrs. Ray told me this memory was wrong. She said I was nowhere before I was born. And I would go there once again someday.

Mrs. Ray said, "You were nothing and you will be nothing again."

Then she laughed giddily.

Further Mrs. Ray told me that, if I had never been born, I would never have minded.

Still, I was very pleased that it had occurred. I kept that to myself. I smiled about it in the dark.

The next time I came back after I had to leave a foster family, Mrs. Ray was away for a vein operation. Another of the Mrs. told me that she was getting a new, special vein put into her hollow leg so that the blood would not clump there like sap on a tree. Several other extra children and I had to make a card for her on newsprint, which the Mrs. stretched out from a roll onto the floor. One of us drew a picture of a purple dragon breathing green fire.

Some time later Mrs. Ray returned from her vein operation. By then I was gone from the holding house already. She visited the place where I was living with my new family, because she had to do what she was prone to call an inspection.

"Well glory, glory be," she said to me, and patted the couch beside her. "This is an awful big cage for a small rat like you. Tee hee."

It was the largest house I had ever lived in up till then, and we each had our own room to sleep in, and there were only two other children besides me. One of them was real. "You know that Jeremy is their actual real son," said Mrs. Ray.

I asked her how her hollow leg was doing after the vein operation. I had thought it was a polite question, but she looked at me with her upper lip tightly wrinkled and the bottom one trembling. She was agitated once again, I could see.

"Who said that, rat?" she asked. "Rat rat rat. Garbage vermin! Stinky!"

The mother of the family was standing behind her at the living room door. And she looked upon Mrs. Ray sternly and told her she was harming my self-esteem as a person. Mrs. Ray went to the bathroom and then left without saying good-bye, but I watched through the front window as she wobbled down the gravel driveway on her square heels. And I felt a sadness descend on me. Her shoulders were hunched over as she went and I wished to tender an apology, although she was too far away already.

So I only said, "Excuse me."

Still, my sadness has never hurt me too badly. That is, if I let it wash over me, I feel newly clean after a while.

It seems only to be the shift of a wind around lost times and opportunities. And I recall the lost things happily and swell in contentment that they ever were. At all.

Anyway.

I plan to travel soon: and I may go back to the nowhere country.

Foot

Sometimes in the bed where I slept with the others, in the waiting place, they would press themselves close on both sides of me. They liked to kick out with their feet and fold my skin in pleats between their hard fingers and fingernails. They called this game the meat sandwich: they were always the bread and I was always the meat. My ribs were crushed in tight when I was the meat, as though my heart would burst.

I thought I must be quite a strange meat, being alive, and not flat, and moving. But then all meat is strange, with the music it sings. There is the dark mass of living things, and then the light that comes from them.

There is even the smallest atom, and the terrible cloud.

Anyway, if the game went long I tended to dream, and the dreams rose like steam around my body.

I dreamed that I was floating on a sea of ink, with the tongues of seaweed curling on my arms and slick black eels flicking and swimming through the holes in me. Since I had seen an eel and a lamprey in two bottles, side by side in a museum to show the difference between them, I had thought of them while asleep. Their blunt heads nudged against me, soft as babies. I dreamed I was burning in a flame of earth, in the mouth of a mountain. I was jostled with sticks, prodded into the ground, stamped down, covered and left beneath the surface.

So I was buried but not without company.

And after a while they would forget the sandwich and nestle, and there was the warmth of them and the salty skin and milky breath. I always have recalled these touches since they were among the first I knew. As for the bruises, shortness of breath and the pressing on me, I think they did not know their own strength.

And some discomfort, like the bites of dogs, was only a small injury. And when we fell asleep together I thought there was no end of us and also no beginning.

. . .

There was a boy named Caesar then, in this large house where on and off we would wait between foster families. And Caesar was the name he gave himself, when he found out about the Romans. He was strong and tall when I was spindly and weak: he had a whole bed for himself. He had suggested this and he was not displeased with the arrangement. After the lights went out the other boys assigned to sleep with him both left his bed, in deference to his largeness. Such great stature requires of course some room for movement.

When morning came they slipped back under the covers with Caesar, before the Mrs. saw.

Sometimes Caesar would mutter to himself, and only I heard him. "They called him the Roman wolf," he would growl, and toss his head in the mirror. Then later he would whisper again: "The Roman wolf, they called him."

Sometimes Caesar would come to me and tap me on the shoulder, and then I gave him all my food. Lickety-split the food was gone, down Caesar's gullet. He liked the yellow pears we each were given on our plates in the fall, juicy and wounded with brown marks on the fat end, and explained how I did not need mine. I was small and thin, he said, but he was not. If you were large, you needed more nourishment, he told me. For example, an elephant could not live on a single peanut for a day, however a sparrow could. Or a mouse, possibly. So he needed my pears more than I did.

At other times Caesar grew weary of the food we were given, because of his discerning palate. Then he went to a market nearby where three streets met, and got food from the merchants.

I asked him how he got it without money, and he said that the merchants worshiped him. First from afar and then up close when they saw how muscles wrapped around his bones and bulged him. They gave him everything he wanted, Caesar said, due to the fact that he was secretly an emperor-prince-king and, in addition, president. But, he said, he was mainly a prince among men.

He came from a tall castle on a tall hill. This castle had towers from whose ramparts black banners unfurled, ends like the tongues of snakes, with Caesar's name emblazoned on them. Princes, Caesar said, took whatever they wanted, and that was how they got it. Besides, like Caesar all of them had one gold tooth. It was a sure sign of a prince.

And I have spotted several in my life.

So when Caesar was hungry, he sought me out; or too he sought me out when all his muscles burst beneath the skin and begged to be employed by him. This was an urge, as he called it. And then he pummeled me. It smarted: yes. Excuse me. I used to think I was a castle too, but a weaker one. A castle made of skin, alive and quavering. Soft flags of blue and yellow would fly on my arms, or a finger would pop with a noise like old crackers.

After the pummelings we were often exhausted, Caesar through being spent in his quite princely energies and me from soreness. So we would both lie on our backs, with legs and hands flung out widely, panting and learning to breathe again. Caesar would not offer up a word of explanation, so I would follow him in silence.

And this is the best part of the memory because there was such harmless quiet, and we gazed up at the trees or roofs and were tired together.

I would be contented in exhaustion.

In fact as I looked up at the sky, in relief I often thought I saw a mother there. She was not a shoebox called *Brown Ladies Narrow 8*, and she was not invisible. Rather she was a coat that covered the earth and made the sun feel softer.

And she said, You are not extra, no. You are good and useful.

Anyway no other children tended to be pummeled by Caesar, since he used all his urges up on me.

After the pummelings I would tend to be absentminded, for a few days at least. On and off, black, purple nets would fall over my eyes, or brown balls of fur roll at the edge of seeing. Science must have a name for these occurrences, but I did not have one. I just recall surprises and mistakes. For instance I was prone to walk in front of vehicles, whose fronts were broad faces with wide silver mouths, headlights for eyes and soft tires for paws. I thought they were animals and could see me equally.

The first time I walked in front of a car, it rolled to a stop accordingly. The second time, we all were leaving to go to the zoo. It was a treat from a nice rich lady who liked panda bears. She also liked emus. We saw a filmstrip that featured her. And she wore very high heels and a long fur coat as she petted a baby monkey.

So she paid for us all to go to the zoo and see them. But excuse me, I never got there.

Because as we were leaving I strolled into the middle of the crosswalk, smiling to myself at a thought I was having about a large dog. But then a car came and had no time to stop. It was moving too fast, and I was churned and twisted. It must have seemed quite comical, since I was a puppet, flailing. One foot of mine was fairly crushed.

When my foot was crushed it was quite an inconvenience for the Mrs. They had to wait on the street with me until the helpful men arrived in their red-and-white van. So finally the class left without me. I apologized to them and to my foot repeatedly, saying, "Oh foot, foot, foot. I'm sorry foot." Later I thought the foot forgave me. Because I wore a stiff boot and slowly it healed, in its wisdom. And now that many years have passed, I have only a slight limp.

But the Mrs. did not. They were angry with me for weeks.

I did not always know that objects only do as they are told and have no will of their own. So the oven made an imprint on my arm, which I still have: two straight bars. I look down at it on occasion and laugh at my stupidity. I knew the oven was hot, but when it burned me I said, "Excuse me." It was only doing its duty, which was to be hot. Anyway, after that I could no longer cook food for the Mrs. One of them said mournfully, "There is no use for you." But as it turned out this was not entirely accurate, for I was competent at scrubbing. And so for years I had that to do.

On another trip after a pummeling, into yellow hills, I made a different kind of error. There was a teacher with us who talked about the parts that make up nature as we went: the grasses and the soils and creatures that inhabit them and go about their business there. However, while we were on a hill some rain began to fall. The sky was close and looming, shot through with lightning in white streaks that shook and then vanished, and tolling deep sounds like massive bells, and I saw it there and wanted to touch it. The others went to stand beneath the trees, but I did not. I thought I could climb up the hill to enter the house of the sky. I would learn later that the sky is never where you are but is always elsewhere.

I ran up the hill to touch the ceiling of the sky, both low and near. But then a shining moment came, and I was covered in brightness.

I thought as I lay there that night had come to me early. As the sun went down the sides of the yellow hills had turned black, and winding among them was an old red train, red the color of rust or earth, snaking beneath the line that cut the hills out of the sky. I could imagine its glowing windows. And the train was carrying my friends, all of them past and far away constantly.

Beyond the mountains and the floodplains were thousands of cities in the night. They were a collar for the black oceans, ringing the continents in shimmers. I thought: My friends live there also. I am sure they do.

I know even now that they do not think of me, and never heard of me at all. But if I could leave this room, we would be reunited.

So I lay on the wet ground on my back and hardly knew how I had gotten that way. Then I smelled the smells of kitchens, when the Mrs. left bread in the oven until it was black, only worse. I touched the top of my scalp, and when my fingers came away they brought hairs with them, singed and dry.

Caesar stood back, laughing. The teacher walked toward me and hoisted me up with his hands underneath my armpits. I stumbled at first and fell backward, but then picked myself up again. Some of the others were laughing and pointing at my head. The teacher shook his head and said I was quite fortunate that I was not deceased.

He said, "You sure are stupid. Why they don't put you with the retards is a mystery."

This was the first time I had heard about my great stupidity. And I was quite surprised, as it had not occurred to me. But certainly it did account for many things. And it always followed a pummeling, when the world blurred into gray edges and my ears throbbed and darted inside. I would wander without destination often, in the wake of beatings. I would believe I was a floating shadow riding on puffs of air, my toes barely skimming the ground.

"Well, that was lightning," said the teacher. "Now you know. Class, what do we know about lightning?" he said, and taught us all about a kite.

Of course I apologized profusely for the bout of stupidity. But I was exhilarated too, and honored since the great black sky had reached to touch me with its hand of light.

Finally, during the winter, some of us were waiting between families for many weeks. Caesar became bored and decided to pummel me. I lay outside a long long time, due to the fact that blood was coming from my head.

So Caesar ran away from me when he noticed. And the red ran away from me too, from inside my nose and also ears, in weaving rivers on the ground. I lay turning my head from side to side slowly, quite curious to see the threads weave and creep and make their thin branches along the gray pavement. And I was so intrigued by these slow trees, I did not notice the cold but just lay there.

I believed there were dents in my head, and that it was caving in. And I would be part of the ground.

So then I caught pneumonia and lay for weeks in a bed all my own, inside a room whose walls were the color of eggshells. No one could visit me except one Mrs. and a minister of God, whom we would all see now and then. He liked to talk of his good friend named Jesus Christ, who sadly died. There is nothing sadder than the death of a dear friend, and I must say the good Father had never fully recovered.

Some of the others were afraid of the Father, in case they had to sit with him alone and on his knees and hear about Jesus in the dark. But I thought he was wise because his face was grave and serious, and I had noticed even then how wise people often assume a very serious aspect, so that their wisdom becomes clear to all others.

I knew while I was sick that Caesar must be hungry for my extra food, and worried a great deal. However I could not see anyone, the Mrs. said, because the sickness might drift out of me and catch the others also. A sickness is alive and only wants to live; a sickness never likes to live alone, but rather is solely happy inside a person or other moving creature, where it finds all its nourishment.

One of the teachers showed us pictures of various sicknesses, and some of them were called bacteria and drawn in diagrams. Some kinds of sickness resemble a necklace of pearls, while others might be the wishbones of a hen. Still others are oval peas in a pod, or silken shoelaces frayed at their ends. The sicknesses are beautiful apparently, but far too small to be seen with bare eyes.

I thought they were frustrated by being so small. And this accounted for their sociability.

Anyway, while I was sick I read books. This was the first time that I saw a book up close, and after that I always loved them and found that they were helpful to improve stupidity. We did not use them in the classes because they cost money, but during the sickness they were brought to me by a woman who was a volunteer. Even the Mrs. could not stop her. She was a Friend of the Library. She brought many, many books, and they were full of words.

She told me all about the library she was a friend of. It had a bird on top for a weather vane, with its wings spread impossibly wide. "Impossibly wide," said the Friend of the Library. "Can you imagine that?"

She said the people at the library would like me, and they would not kick my foot. After she left, I wished she had stayed with me forever.

Instead a Mrs. saw the books and took several away. As it turned out they were terrible filth.

But I felt very fortunate, because before she left, the Friend of the Library taught me to read. And I learned a few words I have liked ever since, and met all the absent friends, who always are everywhere and yet nowhere, leaving their traces in sentences and codes. At first I wished to send letters to them, thanking them for their books. But then it turned out that many of them were already gone. They had slipped away unnoticed.

After I read a book I liked to gaze at the walls endlessly, thinking of the other children, whom I sorely missed. It was true that they were not as fond of me. I had never been at the center since the mangling of my dear foot. Commonly I stood a small ways from the crowd and waited to see whether I was welcome. Presently, Caesar used to approach me and give me a jab.

In spring their chants and games came up through my window in the heat of day, but in the nights only the sky was there and crickets chirping in the grass or a siren whining by on the street like something already forgotten.

I still recall the rain on the evening when the minister came and locked the door and stayed with me. And my window was closed, so I watched the drops on glass as they streamed and joined each other.

The Father put on a play, I think. First he sat on one side of the bed and read from the Jesus book and said a prayer softly. Then he became quite angry, and wrinkles coiled on his face above the eyebrows and around the frowning lips. So then he got up and ran around the bed and sat down on the other side of me and lifted the covers. And then he slapped his own wrist and changed sides again, and read softly about someone who laid with his sister. God was displeased.

Myself, I watched the water, and I watched it. Since then I have always thought water might go anywhere and might do anything.

And I can never know about water.

But anyway, I fell asleep with rivers in my dreams and other dreams of wet bread tearing.

After that I was soon well and went to join the others once again. But Caesar the prince was no longer among them. At first I believed he had been put with a new family, but no family kept Caesar for long. So when he did not come back I grew quite puzzled and concerned. I was afraid he had gone hungry and become smaller and smaller and hid himself from shame for being shrunken.

One of the other children, who slept in the bed with me and made the meat sandwich, said that Caesar had been taken away. I asked her why, and she told me it was due to an occurrence with the merchants. When she said this, the others with us laughed loudly and said it was a lucky circumstance for me. "Little runt."

Still, I was too stupid to know what it meant to be taken away so I asked one of the Mrs. She pursed her lips and said, "Why, Caesar has been moved to a place that is better for him."

I thought about it for some time and then was sure I knew. They finally had found out that Caesar was a secret prince, and had carried him back to the castle, with its great towers and flowing and snapping flags in the wind, where he lived happily.

For some weeks after he left I waited for the mail every day, hoping Caesar would send me a letter on his princely paper stamped with a gold crown. But no letters came, and after a while I saw how foolish I was, since eminent persons cannot trouble themselves with small people such as me. Still I did not forget Caesar, for there was no one else, in those days, who would lie on the ground with me and stare up into trees.

Now when I think of Caesar he is a flash of metal in the sun. Because after Caesar was gone some months elapsed, and even years, in which I was without a friend in those

familiar buildings, though I did so much fetching and bringing for the other children that I was never at loose ends.
And when from time to time I remembered Caesar, I saw
him seated up high upon a graceful throne. And there in
the wide valleys beneath his palace on the hill there were
enormous orchards, where yellow pears grew in profusion.

One day, many years later in a city far away, I was on
the sidewalk of a crowded street. There was a parade of
long black cars in the street, with motorcycles in front
that carried policemen.

I whispered to a woman standing next to me, "What
is this?"

She whispered back, "It is the prince."

And when the longest of the black cars passed, though
the windows were dark too, I thought I saw, for an instant,
the strong face of Caesar.

Caesar was my earliest friend, and if I ever am to see
him once again, and if he has grown old and shrunken by
then and full of shame for being small, I will hold out my
arms and poor Caesar will surely crawl in.

Towel

Once I was lying on the ground, on a frayed orange towel
I had found in a garbage can. I was near the back of the

garden of the apartment that I was then living in, with a chain-link fence beside me that gave onto a dusty alley. Nearby were the remains of a vegetable garden gone wild and a huge lot filled with neat rows of ancient cars in rusting heaps, great boats beached on the burning sand. On their flaking brown bodies, rough to the touch, I sometimes found words in beautiful square scripts that shone as smooth and silver as the day they were born. Eldorado, Mustang, Challenger.

It was in the desert near a highway and the sun was bleaching everything white as a bone in its flat light; but there was a cool breeze rattling the thorny branches of a bush near me. And I had finished all the tasks the mother of the family had given me, so I could rest for a while. I laid my sore legs and arms over the towel, and through the holes the prickly weeds tended to scratch my skin. This made me laugh and scold them.

I was sorry for the weeds because the father of the family hated them. He would always tell me to pull them up so that the grass looked like green felt. He told me weeds were bad and ugly, but I was not sure. I thought that weeds were in the eye of the beholder.

By then I had become less stupid, and I knew that weeds were not known to listen, according to science. But still I did not have the chance to speak with many people, being extra and often not necessary in any given room where people were. So instead I wandered away sometimes and talked to weeds or dirt. The weeds might be listening, I thought, in earless ways, and did not seem to feel too irritated by my voice. At least, so I judged by their patient stillness. But now I know that plants are just polite.

Anyway, I tended to scold the weeds instead of pulling them up as I was told to. I warned them to lie low, so the father would not notice them.

So there I was scolding weeds when a boy from my new school, who never spoke to me normally, came stepping over the brittle leaves of plants. He was large and puffy, with shoulders like a great box and tiny eyes that looked sly because the flesh that sat high on his cheeks pushed them into a squint. He pulled me down onto the ground and draped himself over my person, and went about pursuing an object I was not familiar with. I did not say anything, since he was quite heavy and I was still small and spindly, with my bent foot. So all the air was pressed out of my lungs and none remained to say "Excuse me."

Initially I was confused, but then at last I understood the boy was removing all the space between us. And I thought of all the good and wise other people that he could also have chosen for this, and saw he must be a new friend.

I tried to say something when he raised himself to leave, but he was gruff and turned away and did not look at me again. He only buttoned and went away. I heard him step again on the dry leaves of gone vegetables.

So it was quite a mysterious friendship. Due to all the silence.

There were weeks when I grew tired, because the boy was quick in his closeness and all the force of his limbs, stomachs and shoulders that sank over me, and I was overwhelmed. But I was also grateful, and sometimes even moved to tears, thinking how I was not alone. I had so many tasks at the building where I lived with the foster family that sometimes, when the boy would come to see me, I could not wait for home to rest, but when he went away would fall asleep right there.

I fell asleep against the wall outside the apartment building, on husks of corn I had been carrying inside a paper sack to throw away for the mother. I fell asleep in the bathroom on the floor of tiles in the store where I worked three times a week, which I had been scrubbing with my wet rag beside me and the coarse powder that I used to clean. I fell asleep in the alley with the garbage cans. My cheek might press against cement, my shoulder hunch against a brick, and sleeping I would breathe the dust of floors. In quiet corners I used to wake with the dry taste of dust and feel my throat was full of time.

It was time that lined my nostrils and time that weighed my eyes closed. Sometimes I came awake all worried I had missed my life. In a jolt I felt panic, that somehow I had left myself behind.

But then in relief I would see I was always there, solid and present. And I had not escaped myself by accident.

Still those were strange hot sleeps. And even now, when I smell an egg cracked too long in its carton, I recall the quick closeness of the boy. It was tiring, but I was pleased that he should wish to be near me. Because although the boy hardly said anything, it was so close and so warm, and seemed to be such comfort, that I forgave him for the hastiness. At times a protrusion might cause some discomfort, but I did not mention it. I did not wish him to be embarrassed by the deformity.

I knew about deformities since I now had a foot that was not as footlike as other feet. Still, sometimes it occurred to me, "Why, yes, my foot is a deformity, but I do not place it in other persons' cavities."

I would console myself saying, for all the closeness it is a very small penalty.

And finally I thought: Gone people talk to the living ones in words they leave behind or other things they make. But living ones can talk between themselves more easily, with no words at all. So this is what we are doing. So between the living and the living there is the closeness of skin, the touches that go without words, or past them. Legs go together, stomachs, mouths, cheeks, and finger-tips. The outsides of people push against each other, trying to get in.

And between the living and the gone there are words and colors and buildings. There are footprints, traces, and leavings.

And between the gone and the gone, it is impossible to know if they use words or are so close they do not need them.

Trying to make the squinting boy feel better, I said, "Don't worry, don't worry," but he only breathed heavily.

I whispered, "We can be closer than words, but not closer than skin."

Then he put his moist palm on my mouth to stop me talking, and the edge of my front teeth made a ridge in the inside of my lip.

And that was when I first understood injuries, and persons who cause them. These persons are warriors. They will not be stopped by skin. It is no barrier to them: they wish to conquer it. They will tear it off, even, to get closer in.

I think they want to catch the soul. They think that souls are heart and bone, residing in a certain place, and can be known by traveling.

He would never cease wanting, and he would never cease trying. Because of that I loved him.

*When I was a little older I would take trips to visit van*ished people in their gardens of neglect. I went to see them in the country, where a low wind may blow over the stones and dandelions grow through the cracks, or even willow roots or the flat white parasols called Queen Anne's lace.

In cities old papers, cups, and other used-up objects gather on the fences and beneath the edges of the written stones, and make the cemeteries feel like casual places for discarded things. I always liked to go there anyway, and pick up trash, and read the writing on the graves. I liked to invent memories of those who had vanished underneath the grass.

I often thought about the gone.

In any case, one day the stern man who was the principal of the school came into the back lot and saw the boy and me. I recollect it well because my eyes were wide open as the boy was pressing me down. There was no towel beneath us, so the weeds were in my back, boring small holes there with their spines, while the boy rocked back and forth and I was in the shape of a cradle.

I looked up and saw the long wings of a bird above us, and then the principal's face, which seemed enormous since it was so near. I smiled at him, but the stern principal was not prone to smile.

He was polite then, plantlike. He did not speak or move to interrupt the boy but stood above us, gazing and gazing until the boy got tired and slumped on me. I always knew when it was coming to an end, for I was always watching as if I were not there at all: I rose like a periscope through air and saw myself beneath me, pinned by a giant boy. Our limbs looked white and tubular, the tentacles of unknown entities. We were jellyfish, luminous in the deep. I did not mind our alien qualities, in fact they filled me with joy. I thought: How lucky we are. Unlike the weeds we move freely.

The principal mostly gazed at me but not my face; he pressed his lips together, and sometimes he would blink for a long moment. When the boy was quiet and still before he raised himself to go away, the stern principal, soundless, also faded.

I think the sun was burning his dear eyes.

Tooth

However, the next day the principal called me into his office. He sprayed his metal desk with blue solution from a bottle, wiped it with a paper towel, and told me to sit down. He bunched the paper towel and threw it into a wire basket and sat down himself. Then he looked at me across the smooth top of the desk. He drummed his fingers on the surface and the nails made a quick clicking sound. I stared at them and saw they were sharp.

Then he cleared his throat and said I had to leave. I said, "Excuse me?" This was the longest I had ever been in a school. I did not know then, as it happened, that I was not going to see the rows of vegetables or ancient cars again, or the desert that laked the highway. Back then I did not know that things went forward forever and left older things behind. I did not know that things ended but only felt them pass in shapes and flights; I was flung and turned in waves and lulls, and the lines between things were not clear.

As the memories collected in me, as they have in you I am sure, I discerned a past and also a future. But still I do not always know the difference too acutely, since dreams seep into memory, or memory into a dream.

Until recently I did not know if the future would end. I thought that maybe, like the sky, it was out of reach at all times and yet always persisting.

. . .

I recall clearly the last night I spent with the other chil-
dren of the foster family. They were angry, though I did not
know why. They told me that they knew about me, what I
was and why I had to leave the school and all of them
behind. "You little slut!" they said. "You stupid, stupid slut."

But this word was not in any of the books that had
been brought to me by the Friend of the Library. "Excuse
me," I said.

Still, they did not excuse me; rather they squeezed me
more than usual, with hands in my hair, knocking against
my lips and teeth and pulling the skin of my arms and my
cheeks. I said, "Excuse me" several times again, and apologized once more, but it did not appear to matter what I
said, for their distress and agitation were quite evident.

When they had finished they let me rest beside the
bed, on the floor. And again it was fortunate that they
asked me to roll off the bed, with their eager, pushing
limbs, because while I was there I located a tooth from
my mouth. It was one from the back. I felt its sharpness
underneath my fingers and knew what it was right away.
It had gone missing just a few minutes previously. I could
not put it back in its hole, but I have kept it with me to
this day, to remember the last meat sandwich.

They surely meant no harm, but like so many who are
moved by will, such as Caesar, they must not have known
their own strength.

After they left me to rest down on the floor, which I had just swept and scrubbed so it was clean, they felt much better and laughed together in the dark until they fell asleep.

I wondered then if I had been a stupid, stupid slut. I wished to be a wiser one, certainly.

Yet I have found that wise people may err on the side of caution. Some have advised me to avoid large dogs, in case they bite, for example. But I like to touch a large dog, to glide my hand over the fur and breadth of the bone. If I were ever bitten by a large dog, I would certainly laugh but I would not regret it. For all the large dogs I have touched one bite would be a small penalty. And sometimes I remember the large squinting boy and the minutes of him, and the others who did not know their own strength. And I feel fortunate after all. Because I had the privilege of knowing him, and all of them, before they were all gone.

So I could not take all the advice I received, even then. I know it is often very good, but back then, as also later in my life, when I was old, the sheer volume could be overwhelming.

People are generous with their wisdom, I have found. They distribute it willy-nilly, in acts of great charity.

Due to the twinges, I did not sleep easily myself. I chose to stand up in the dark and walk to the bathroom we shared. And there I used the time I could not sleep to wash the various abrasions that I had. One of my eyes stayed closed, but I could see well through the other. However, at certain moments over the next few weeks I would lose my balance in a comical fashion, and stumble foolishly.

As I lay on the floor beside the bed, after I had cleaned my scrapes, I dreamed a dream I had not dreamed before. I dreamed I was awake and wandered through the house, where all the others I knew were sleeping. And I went to each bed and to each person in those beds and looked at them. And each one I touched above their eyes. There was the mother with the pink rash on her forearms and her boyfriend with his earring in the shape of a leaf. He breathed like a snuffling pig while he slept and I was concerned he would not get enough air, for his nostrils were thin as toothpicks. There was the real daughter, with a china horse beside her bed.

When I was done, stealthy in the dream, a discomfort crept over me. At first I could not pinpoint the source of it, until I remembered that my fingertips were full of cracks, and leaking.

And so on every head, there on the skin over the eyes, by accident, there was a watery red smear. Which was rude, and also quite impolite.

I became sad and worried, as I lay there clenching my tooth in my hand, that all the people would find out that I had gone near them while they slept, and turn on me angrily. For being such a slut. So I got up again and went to find wet cloths. And I went back to each of them and drew the cloths across the skin, and made the marks invisible again.

Still I knew it was only a dream, for I would never have been so bold.

2

Long before the building fell silent, I already knew my floor well. In the days when Jim the night orderly brought in food on a brown tray for me, I was learning each rub and scuff and every crescent where a chair or a heel had dug in. Even sleeping I could have drawn you a map. There was nowhere I could put my eyes but the floor, the walls, and the ceiling.

First thing in the morning, Jim brought me oatmeal in milk, and a half peach with syrup in a plastic bowl. It was always the same bowl, or at least it was a series of identical bowls, pink and dull from years of washing. There were no forks or knives, since I was only allowed to eat soft food. I might do violence to my person, they said. Due to being unhinged, apparently. Without hinges, a door cannot open or shut but abandons its axis and dangles wantonly.

I grew to be very fond of the floor, though I could not say why exactly. In confinement, even with an object such as gray linoleum, I found there was a love of abject things. We kept each other company. And though the linoleum would stay the same insistently, seemingly unfeeling, its quietness did not bother me.

I wanted to help the linoleum. But there was nothing I could do for it.

I would think of all the people outside who had graceful lands in plain view, purple mountains looming over the desert with thunderclouds crowning them, or narrow streets with a salt breeze in a city by the sea. I would remind myself of the days when I had been outside too, barely noticing anything, it now seemed to me. And I wondered what kingdoms had passed me unseen.

Jim the night orderly liked to say I was not missing anything. When I asked him about the wind or the sky he would always shrug and say "I dunno." When I asked him if it was warm or cold or clear or raining, he would also shrug and say "I dunno." When I asked him about the city he would shrug and say, "Sleaze, bag ladies, and sin."

He did not mean it as a compliment.

But I thought of the city as he described it, and I saw armies of bag ladies and they looked good to me.

So even before the silence, I was kept in this locked room and held to be quite severely unhinged. I could not leave the room except at certain hours, maybe two or three times a month when Jim, before he went home, had time to take me. And these were hours in which the corridors were empty. Through the dirty glass of the tall windows, the light of dawn was tired and made the white floors blue. Along these shining blue-white halls I would shuffle in the cold sunrise with Jim beside me.

Presently we would emerge.

And there Jim would allow me to stand for fifteen minutes, on a small fenced balcony overlooking a parking lot. On the balcony beside me were several ashtrays like flowerpots, growing white and caramel stumps in their beds of sand.

I was often overcome. Around the edge of the parking lot were thin shrubs and spindly trees that trembled with the fullness of themselves. I saw the details of their leaves, their shades fading into each other and their lovely and tangled anatomies. I was used to flat surfaces and blank walls by then.

And there above us was the sky in glory, and behind it invisible the rest of the universe, which later, science would say, might be expanding into infinity.

And all its atoms spread so thin they disappeared.

Whether or not this is the case, it certainly was more infinite than I could see. At the end of the universe, outside the end of everything, what nothing would be has always been beyond me. I never could understand it. But all through my happy life there has been no better thought than to try. The end of the universe and being gone, both of them forever.

Anyway, after fifteen minutes, when Jim had smoked his two cigarettes, it was inside again for me.

"Hop hop hop," Jim would say. "Before anyone sees."

So twice a month I got to leave my room behind, and leave the walls, and corners, and plaster, and the artificial lights and metal furniture. I got to abandon squareness, which is not a shape that happens often of its own accord, except in crystals growing beneath the scale of sight. I could forget edges and corners and only remember bursting and trailing forms. Back then I wanted more time on the balcony, and sometimes I would ask Jim if he would take me out more often. He would nod then and say, "Sure, sure, sure." And I would be thrilled as I saw the prospect of more time spread before me. I thought: Every day. Twice a day. Or even at night, and I will learn the constellations.

I would plan to see airplanes with blinking lights descending to the city. I would also plan to see orange comets trailing across the black velvet, fireworks bursting pink and yellow, bats flitting and owls swooping and the faint white smudge of many billions of stars in the spiral galaxy.

But Jim was always too busy.

And now I often see a figment of Jim. He stands at my open door holding two cigarettes. And I think there is no difference between two cigarettes and freedom.

After those times and for the rest of the day, smiling, I used to walk around and around in my room, turning and roaming repeatedly. And I would gaze at the spread of gray linoleum between my feet as though it were remote as the moon, even a foreign moon, a distant satellite of a planet I would never be certain existed. It was furrowed with ridges, craters, flecks, and scars; it flickered with the occasional shadow of a footstep, in the form of a dim column, barely perceptible, slanting under the door and then moving away. Similarly a bank of clouds tends to darken a field as it passes.

So the floor was a country all its own; it had the suggestion of a past, the hint of a future, and signs of habitation by those whom I did not know.

And this was all I needed to imagine a microscopic yet vast colony spread out across the valley of my floor, too small for clumsy eyes.

I was not wrong, I believe. But the continent remains unknown to me.

The last time I was led onto the balcony by Jim the night orderly there were yellow giants scooping deep maws of gravel from the parking lot with their claws. The concrete had been broken everywhere, and the cars that used to be parked there were all gone. I asked what the machines were doing, and Jim said, "They're shutting us down. Sold the lot to a developer."

He stubbed out his cigarette and then he said, "Anyway. I gotta new job; I'm outta here on Friday."

I remember this perfectly because it was the last thing that was ever said to me. And save for one more bowl of oatmeal, maple and brown sugar flavor, which was delivered through a slot in my door the next morning, it was the last I saw of anything outside the room. I think when Jim went to his new job he must have taken with him all memory of me. As there was none of it left behind. Apparently.

It seems like years ago, but surely it was only a number of weeks.

Happily I still have sleep, and still have my soft memories. Someone wise once told me that memory could be divided into near and far categories, but for me the kinds of memory are hard and soft. Soft comes by itself, slipping in through the curtains in rays and slanting or beaming across empty floors suddenly, breaking the dark. Whereas hard memories are assignments. Remembering some rules is hard, and times and procedures, and the numbers that people are given in long sequences of digits. I have had little understanding of numbers, in my life. It has caused some problems.

Money always has escaped me and in turn, without wishing to I promise, I have escaped the kindness of the state. From time to time. But kindness always finds me in the end.

Back then, when I was young, events were like soft memories are now. In fact I cannot say for sure that those events I am recounting, of all my life before this room, were not just always memories themselves, given to me along with my toenails or eardrums, as a gift.

And sleep leaches soft memories into my body. I get heavy with them. I am suspended and lazy in a hammock, and they fall over me. Or I am in a cubbyhole in a treehouse, warm dark wood full of eyes sprouting out of the soil.

Some people do not hold sleep in high regard; they have many obligations for which to remain wide awake and vigilant, sitting, walking, and enumerating. They are in charge, they have lists and plans.

I am in charge of nothing.

But anyway, in sleep there are nothing but soft memories. So I have always welcomed it, floating on the rim of green and clear seas, a gentle skin of waves holding me up. I know I should not fear sinking. And I can only guess at the fathoms of water beneath me, with their trailing plants and coral and the far-off slow solid currents of lava in tall black columns underneath, as they stretch out of rift valleys, so far beneath that no one reaches them.

Or too, in sleep I have wings like the great white bird, felt but not seen, that propel me upward on pillars of wind. And then without weight or shells, wheels or engines all of us swoop together in updrafts and downdrafts above the sloping fields and glittering rivers through the lands. Beneath us are the wild forests, the shaded gardens and small curving roads that we would wish to see, as if our thoughts had made them rather than history. In perfect sway they unroll endlessly.

So there the air is also ours for moving through, the air and the ocean beneath, and nowhere is impossibility.

It is a great luxury. Sometimes I have heard that people who have to work all the time with their hands or on their feet never get enough sleep, and also tend to forget their dreams. Or possibly they cannot feel the dreaming.

I have put my box, my towel, and my tooth all in one corner for now, in a neat pile. I am trying to separate all the parts of my life, one per wall until all four walls are covered with the scribble of it. There is not even toothpaste left now, and it has become apparent to me that the difference between being and not being at all may be as small as half a peach.

Frilly Ear

The inside of ears is a sculpture of bones, romantic like the curves of flowers. A cochlea curls in on itself like a snail shell, a malleus and incus look like a cowskull, everything is like something else. I learned these names from the encyclopedia. There was a black-and-white diagram in the encyclopedia, of all the pieces of a person's brain, and all the wondrous organs that tell the brain the world. There I saw that my head was a hive of activity, in which many things are certainly arranged without my knowledge.

The outside of an ear is only less strange because it is so often seen.

In the house where I worked after leaving the Mrs., where they sent me, we all had tasks, except for the woman and the man whose house it was. Their job was to think of the tasks, then lie down. My own tasks in the house were told to me by a very large friend who was named Désirée. She was born in a quiet place with sunny weather, she told me, and also many times she told me how she was named for the secret true love of an emperor, long ago.

But she herself was not the secret true love of an old emperor. Instead she was the secret true love of her very small husband.

The small husband of Désirée lent his assistance when he gathered leaves from off the lawns, in fall, and cut the grass, in summer and in spring. He had his own truck the color of clay, and in the back he kept all manner of machines, whose handles stuck up in the bed of the truck like a forest of metal trees. I met him several evenings when he came to the door that led from the driveway. That was the door for us, but not for the man and woman of the house.

Anyway, whenever I would see and speak with the small husband of large Désirée, he was always quite happy, having consumed a vast array of fine intoxicants.

Numerous people, in their wisdom, are happiest when drinking such a vast array. Of course they like the light— golden from whiskey, yellow from beer, or red from wine— in which they bask as though it were the sun.

But Désirée would cluck her tongue and pick up her very small husband by the scruff of his neck like a cat. She would drag him back to his truck, and then she would drive him home. She did not live in the basement of the big house like me. Therefore she did not sleep on a cool slim cot in the room with the furnace, or have the pleasure of the gray mice that ran and scampered there, or of the small brown cockroaches, as ancient as the dinosaurs, that nestled in the cracks of the walls and also scampered when they felt like it. And that was fine with her because she did not like the dinosaurs and would descend and flatten them with the spatula she used for scrambled eggs. Prior to this action she would scream out "Cucaracha!"

I said, "Poor dinosaurs." Because they only went about their business as they thought they should. They were not overly wise: they never learned about the spatula. I once saw a small dinosaur escape, but he did not convey a warning to his friends.

Other people also lent assistance with us in the big house, and also slept in the rooms of the basement. There was Brad who drove the large and shining car for the man and the woman, and Louise who sat and typed on a machine for the woman. She never liked to speak with me, because she was too wise. I admired her but she had many tasks, and could not often stay and talk with Désirée and me. Brad's car went everywhere with the man and also with the woman, when she had to go away and bring back bags and carry them up to her private bedroom. I was never asked to go to clean in there, because it was so private. But sometimes Brad would carry all the bags for her, when they were heavy, and then they would both go inside her room and close the door behind them and lock it, so the room was not private to Brad.

However it was private to the man of the house, because he had to knock before he went in. Late at night sometimes he knocked, and then there was no answer and he went away.

No room was private for Oscar the Pekingese dog. This Pekingese dog, which Désirée always called "the Pekingese dog" though his real name was Oscar, belonged to the woman of the house, who liked to carry Oscar wherever she had to go. She called him Oscar at times, and at other times "my pedigree Pekingese." Often the woman would have Oscar the pedigree Pekingese on one arm and a shopping bag on the other.

I was always glad to have my day off on Sunday, because I could then walk through the streets and speak to people. And I kept my towel, which I took with me and spread out on the grass in one park or another. And I could go to the library to visit all the vanished ones, or walk to schools and gaze at all the empty buildings of the schools, or sit in playgrounds swinging slowly on a swing. I would see other people there, smaller ones than me, with their mothers and fathers, who would say to me, "Well, why aren't you in school?"

And I would mumble and go away.

There was no time for me to go to school then, due to all the tasks I had. But I would often think of school. I thought of the rooms with teachers at the front and all the students looking at them.

Because I could not go to school, I decided to read more books. However many of the books at the new library were not too wise but rather shiny on the front with big silver or gold writing. These books could be used to see with in the dark. All books are good and useful.

Sunday was also the day when Désirée went home, so sometimes on Sundays there was no food for me. The man and woman of the house did provide funds in return for my assistance, but these went into a small booklet with a row of numbers stamped across the top. I never held the funds myself or knew how much they were, because the woman kept the booklet safe in a cabinet she locked with a key.

Then it came to pass that Désirée's small husband drove his truck into the driveway one fine summer evening. But excuse me: under the front tire was Oscar.

The woman became very angry, since she was so sad, about this Pekingese dog, which certainly was flattened by the tire of Désirée's small husband's truck.

And Désirée's small husband cried and cried, and said that he was sorry, having drunk once more a fine array. And he was weeping so loudly and so sadly that I cried too, for Oscar and also for him. He had always had a fondness for Oscar, even though he was never allowed to touch him or pet him either. But he always used to wink at Oscar, and also shake his head smiling when Oscar trotted past wearing pink bows.

The woman of the house pushed him away and said that Désirée would also have to go and not come back. So Désirée chose to be angry too, because she had a temper, as she liked to say to me. She put her husband in the truck, still weeping with his very small shoulders shaking. And all the while little Oscar, the Pekingese dog, was still lying there beneath the tire.

Désirée looked at the woman of the house and drove off Oscar and then drove over him again. And I was watching from behind the screen of our own kitchen door and heard the woman shriek and scream. But Désirée did not seem to be concerned about the shrieking and drove over Oscar several times until he was so flat I could not see him anymore.

And then she kept on driving and drove away.

I became sad, knowing I would not see my dear friend Désirée again. Some hours went by and I was asked to clean up Oscar. And while I shoveled Oscar I was still so sad that I did not see Oscar as I cleaned him up, because of all the weeping, and I turned my face away and pretended to be blind. And I did not look at the remains of Oscar. Oscar was very flat indeed. And anyone who saw him at that time would not know that he was a pedigree Pekingese.

This was when I learned how people might become gone instantly. Oscar had quickly become deceased, so that, when flattened several times again, he did not mind. The woman of the house said, "He is dead, dead, dead!"

Later she said several times that Désirée should also die, die, die.

Soon after that the woman brought another cook to do what Désirée had done, and she was very kind but left quite soon. And there were quite a few cooks who came and went, and though they were all wise and kind they never stayed too long. The man of the house went on numerous trips, and the woman of the house, who went and bought herself a new pedigree Pekingese, called Oscar Too on a tag that hung around his neck, also began to drink a vast array of fine intoxicants.

Brad grew kind to me and sometimes spoke to me in the driveway while he was polishing the car. I liked him very much and certainly enjoyed hearing him speak about the car, and other cars that he admired. Sometimes he also spoke about his plans to buy an excellent and lovely car, and drive it all around. But other times he only spoke about the cars he did not have.

One day he put me on his back and ran around the yard. However then the woman of the house came out and saw us running there and threw a bottle of intoxicants at Brad. It did not hit us but rolled slowly on the grass.

So then she went inside again.

After some days she called me to her private room, which I had never seen before. And in the bedroom with its carpet of red velvet she took a pink stick that she usually used to draw on her lips. And she wrote with it on the wall and then said, "Wipe it up." She wrote her name eight times, until the pink stick was used up, as well as two orange sticks and a red. Then she sighed and took a bath. And told me to clean up the writing with my sponge.

It was remembering this that gave me the idea to write on my own walls, so I am grateful.

However, it would not come off entirely, and so she got new wallpaper.

After that she often chose to follow me throughout the house as I performed my tasks. Wherever I was tidying she liked to sit and pour a substance on the floor, or break a glass, and then five more. And when I finished for the day, she called me to her room and sometimes locked the door, and then she ate some of her supper there and threw the rest onto the bed, or she would tear a shiny book apart and drop its pieces into the sink, or bath, or the washing machine. She also liked to heave a potted tree across the room.

She would say, "Dirty dirty! Clean it!"

So I grew tired increasingly, for even when I slept she sometimes came to me and sprinkled powder all around my bed, or tore apart a bag of rice and flung it through the halls. It was when I was sleeping that she came one night and took hold of my ear, and pulled me upward by the ear while I was still asleep. This caused the ear to tear like cloth, and I woke up. And there was warmth on my neck, and the dark air in the basement rolled with fiery wheels. And my poor earlobe was in the woman's right hand. So she screamed.

However, I have always had good fortune, certainly undeserved. For while the ear was healing, wrapped in gauze and black electrical tape Louise had found in a drawer, the man returned from a long business trip. And he had scarcely been home for five minutes when some other men came in too. Several came creeping in the kitchen door in uniforms, holding their fingers to their lips. This made me laugh as I recalled the boy at school.

They went through the kitchen then and stamped and tumbled up and down the stairs with the man of the house, and took him out the door again and sat him in their car and drove away. And then another man came from the bank and talked quite solemnly to the woman of the house and said she could not live there anymore. While this was taking place Brad, Louise, and the cook put several objects from the house in plastic bags, to take away themselves as souvenirs, such as the silver forks and knives, a small television, and a radio. Then they went out the kitchen door and disappeared.

And then some other men came in and watched the woman of the house pack clothing into suitcases, but did not let her pack her jewelry. And so she left with her two suitcases and Oscar Too.

The other men took all the furniture and lamps made of fat gold angels, and rugs and paintings too, and almost every item that was in the house, and put it all in an enormous truck, and then a second truck, because there were so many things.

But all this time no one said much to me. No one folded and carted away my cot from the basement, as they did the great brass beds from upstairs. No one removed the cans of food from the basement or my gray mice or the dinosaurs. So when upstairs was empty and every room was bare, I cleaned and tidied the footprints from the tiles and the carpets and then went down to the basement. It was still cool and dark.

Leaf

I lived in the basement for several months without tasks, eating food from cans and sleeping whenever I wished to. No one was telling me what to do, so the days had a strange looseness to them. I had never lived without tasks and at first I did not know how, so I impersonated animals.

For instance I pretended to hibernate, bearlike; or I beetled along the rims of cracks in the ground, sneaking between other people's houses and scavenging for sounds and evidence of them. This was best practiced at sunset or by moonlight. I could not be seen, I thought, and now and then music or a sudden snippet of voice would float across the dark. Then, retreating to my cool space underground, I could lie down, close my eyes, and rifle through the tracings on the backs of my eyelids.

Mrs. Salinas, one mailbox said. She was squat, with hair that was black on the top of her head and light yellow at the ends, and wore many long bead necklaces that swung and rattled when she walked. She paced around her dining room table almost every night when she finished eating, clucking and shaking her head. Sometimes she wore a baseball cap backward. Then she tended to stop and stare at the table, reach out and grab the candlesticks from the centerpiece, sit down on a chair, and play on an invisible drum.

Beside where I lived, in a big house with a porch, lived a family. There was a girl around the same size as me, and her younger sister. The younger sister's bedroom was on the ground floor. So sometimes I hunched silent at the bottom of her window. She liked to talk on a plastic toy telephone, saying, "Yes, I would *love* to go out with you, Davy! Marry you? Why *yes!*" She did headstands so her skirt fell over her head, and stretched her face into contortions in front of the mirror.

The older sister was pale, with brown eyes and brown hair.

I was curious to know them, but I did not want Protective Services to discover me. So I impersonated a bat and flapped off into the shadows.

Farther afield there was a window that held a man and a woman, always fighting. They fought in a room with a couch, a globe of the world that was caved in on one side, and a brand-new television that lit the room blue. The man had a very long head, shaped like an eggplant, and the woman had nearly gray skin. Once she was sitting beside the man on the couch, watching television, when she pulled a tiny white box from her apron pocket. From the box she unspooled a long, white thread. This she put in her mouth, sliding it between her teeth and then pulling it back and forth.

The man said, "Could you stop that?"

But she kept on pulling it and did not answer. Finally he stood up and slouched away.

After a while I decided that if I went far enough away from my basement, from the concrete floor that sank in the middle into a rusted drain, the small piles of books and objects that belonged to me, and any sign of Protective Services, then I could move among crowds. Possibly one time I would even speak to people, if they let me. So I started to wander to the celebrations of strangers.

I would walk aimlessly throughout the afternoon and the early evening, going nowhere but ending by arriving. Festivities were always springing up like new shoots. Both the women and the men tended to smile as they consumed intoxicants. When they consumed intoxicants they laughed, stumbled, and landed on each other, reminding me fondly of the small husband. I gathered quickly that people had warm opinions when they drank golden drinks: then they forgot all their opinions after a time had passed. They let go of the wisdom that had become such a burden and kept them apart. The liquid of them flowed together.

The first such celebration I happened onto was the wedding of two persons I had never met. It took place on a lawn in the spring. There were bushes thick with buds and shining leaves, the grass was freshly mowed, and there were sparkling glasses and a tall cake like a white building. All the smiling persons were clothed in finery. I would have faded in since no one was looking at me, only I got overwhelmed during the ceremony and fell down quite suddenly. I slid to the ground behind a stone bench.

I fainted again while I was watching the dancing, and several people saw me. It was quite an imposition, and I was embarrassed as they leaned over me, peering. I felt ashamed. As soon as my head had stopped swimming I left stealthily.

There were so many, all at once smiling and open, and with bright shining clothes and silken bags with jewels on them and necklaces and rings and slick sparkling shoes. And they gleamed everywhere around me, brightly.

At one party I wandered to on a Sunday evening in summer, I sat down at a table across from an ancient woman. There were streamers dangling from the branches of trees and glass bowls full of punch with thin orange slices. Presently I looked at this old woman and I saw that she was crying without even moving her face. I had not spoken to her, and still I did not say a word. But we were both sitting at the picnic table, which was covered in a checkered cloth of red and white.

The tears came from her eyes and ran down her cheeks and fell onto the red and also onto the white, where I observed them. She was resting her wrinkled elbows on the tabletop. Around us there were people dancing slowly with their arms on each other's shoulders and waists.

All the people dancing were quite ancient, for the party was outside a building where only ancient people lived.

Finally I started crying too.

This went on for a few minutes, until the old woman stopped crying herself and reached across the table.

"We're not alone," she said.

Then she said she was tired and asked me to come inside and put her to bed. She had a room that she said was her home. In her room she lay down on her back, with her head propped up on some pillows. I sat on a chair beside her. I saw there was a stuffed animal on the bedside table, and it was a camel. It too was ancient, of threadbare blue plaid and with the stuffing coming out. I looked out her window and I thought that such a vastness as the sky would take us all in, for there was plenty of room.

Just when I thought she was falling asleep, she said, "Would you like to see a trick?"

I said yes. So she held out her right wrist and told me to place my fingers there, on the vein.

"You feel that?" she asked, and I nodded. "That's my pulse, my heartbeat. Keep your fingers on it and you'll see."

She closed her eyes. So we were peaceful there, waiting and not waiting. After a while I forgot about the trick and looked out the window at the stars again. I considered galaxies, which I had read about. Next I considered dusty brown planets, where three yellow moons hung low in the sky and the purple seas lapped warm and soft. I certainly hoped that such planets existed. The woman's hand became heavy. I was thinking of also going to sleep, curling up on the bed at her feet, when I noticed the flicker of her pulse was gone.

I asked, "Is that the trick?"

I looked at her for a long time, but there was no answer. So I crept away.

Sometimes I would steal up from my basement to the second floor of the house. There was a window there from which I could watch the street. I could see the girls from the house with the porch as they ran down the street trailing thin voices behind them or jumped through the weaving sprinkler on their wide lawn.

On this lawn was a ginkgo tree, of a kind that had lived for hundreds of millions of years. I picked up a leaf from the tree and stored it between the pages of a book until it was dry.

And then one evening I caught sight of the warm orange light from a window in the house with the porch, and so I crept over across the grass to look inside. There was a dining room with a wooden table and a chandelier that hung overhead, diamonds winking. And the family was eating dinner. They cut their food busily with knives while the father was talking. Behind them there was a painting on the wall of a family that looked just like them.

The father had a mustache and chewed potatoes, shaking his head now and then. The mother pushed asparagus to and fro on her plate with her fork. The girls jiggled their legs under the table, and the older one, who was facing me, pulled her bottom eyelids down to show the pink part and then pushed the tip of her nose up to look like a pig.

Her mother and father did not notice this. And the younger sister was dropping food on the rug for a cat.

But I laughed harder than ever before. It was the funniest. I rocked and turned around and bent forward shaking, and finally I went back to the window. But she did not make the pigface again.

So I decided to make the pigface myself and see if anyone would notice me. And I stood there for quite some time with the pink part of my bottom eyelids meeting the air and my nose pushed up. Soon my eyes were watering, and tears were streaming down beside my piglike nose. However, I persisted and pushed my face nearer the windowpane.

That was when the brown-haired girl saw me and screamed.

I screamed too and sprang back from the window. And then I ran away fast, and behind me I heard the front door opening. Big feet stamped over the porch.

But the sun had already set, and they lost sight of me in the dark.

The day after, she came and found me in the basement. She said she had seen me before. She promised not to tell Protective Services. I said, "Or your parents either?" She said, "My dad said it was a prowler. But my mom said rapist."

So we would meet in secret places after that. We left notes in tin cans for each other. Her name was Amanda. Once she put a note in a cat food can, and it smelled very bad. But I was happy to get it anyway. It said: "MeAT me in the pARK!!! 4 pM!"

She pretended I was a pirate, or sometimes we were both outlaws on the run. Protective Services was looking for us. They would lock us up, she said, and throw away the key. They might also gun us down like robbers.

At night we would signal to each other across the yard, me in the bedroom upstairs, where the woman of the house used to sleep, and she in her own bedroom. I used a flashlight that belonged to her father. We learned Morse code and used it to talk at night. She once signaled to me: "XOXO. You Are FrieD."

That was proof.

And once, in a thunderstorm when the ginkgo tree fluttered and swayed, after she went to sleep, I clutched my blanket around me and looked out the window and felt safe. I peered through the sheets of rain and thought I could still see Amanda at her window, waving to me out of her lighted room. All over the vast land, I knew then, there were rooms just like this, and people enclosed within them warm and dry.

I thought: What if I was wise and lucky enough to have some friends and live with them. And what if we were happy there, and people chose what they would do all day. I thought, What if we knew that all the others were safe, too, and were so glad they came and went upon the earth that we were not even afraid to die, die, die.

Reeds

I had to leave the house presently. Before the sold sign went up, I heard people talking as they tapped across the floor above me in their hard heels. "I knew this place was you the first time I saw it," said a woman with a bold and carrying voice.

So then I said good-bye to Amanda.

After I left the house I slept in a park under one or another tree, or sometimes even in a tree. One of them had a broad flat bough that arched up very gently, a wide-spread arm.

The park was in a quiet, neat part of the city, surrounded by tidy square shops and restaurants. I used to wake up as soon as the sky was light and go to scrub the tiles or ovens or carry food or newspapers for people who worked in the stores, restaurants, or bakeries. They would offer me a plate of food someone had not finished, or a stiff loaf of bread.

And in exchange for living in the park beneath the trees, I picked up things that visitors had left. Bottles, wrappers, and cups were common, or sometimes, in the mornings, old wet white balloons. These were always deflated and I wondered where they came from, if they fell to earth in a flock, shot down by hunters, or drifted from the clouds like snow to settle in bald patches in the grass and under benches.

I placed all of these things in the cans reserved for items that had already served their purpose well. One day in such a can I found a raincoat that snapped together at the front, which I hung above me like a roof. It was perfectly clear, so when it rained I lived inside a glass house. And there was a barber who let me wash myself in his deep sink at night. I would sweep cut hair from off the floor and then bend down over the sink and let hot water from the spigot run over the back of my neck and down the long dent of my spine.

I liked the black padded chairs in a row and the dark hush of a place where all day long men had sat patiently.

Once in the afternoon, while I was raking a lawn for cigarette ends, I felt a hand on my shoulder, and I looked at the thick and puffy fingers and then a bulbous gold watch and an arm in a dark blue suit. And I saw the person who commanded them. It was an old man with a nose like a purple flower.

He asked me where I lived, and I said in a tree. He

laughed and said, "Which tree?" So I took him to the tree and showed him how I climbed, favoring the weak foot, and how I stretched out on the wide limb that grew almost parallel to the ground, and could sleep there comfortably.

I also showed him the clear raincoat.

But he grew displeased, shaking his head and saying people could not sleep in trees. For a moment I was afraid he was Protective Services. So I clambered down and tried to walk away in a hurry, but he came quickly after me, still talking.

Anyway, this old man visited me every day for a while and would bring me a sandwich or a bar of chocolate containing nuts, and give it to me while sitting on the bench smiling and nodding at me. And he would eat a chocolate bar himself, peeling the paper back bit by bit like a banana peel as he nibbled it down. But even then, as he nibbled away cautiously, his eyes were prone to follow me.

And finally this man, Mr. D., said I should leave the tree and stay in rooms that he furnished. They were warm in the winter and cool in the summer, he said.

It was the opposite of the world.

But Mr. D. was insistent.

So I went there, and I found a room with pink walls, a rocking chair, a soft bed, and a blanket. There were even two blankets there, even three. I could pull them up to my chin and feel welcome.

As it happened, Mr. D. was not with Protective Services, but still I thought he might call them if I went back to the park and the tree. Once I even asked him if he would. He shook his head slowly, but it seemed to me that as he did so he was also nodding.

Then Mr. D. brought many plants into the room, which he told me were a little bit of nature. They had shining leaves and large flowers, and some of them even had teeth and ate flies. He also brought dolls to me, which I did not prefer. They had fat rosy cheeks and long eyelashes. In the dark I thought they were smiling at me, and I would burrow deeper beneath my blankets.

I was not sure what to do. Mr. D. was friendly, but not like a friend precisely.

And soon he brought a tool into the room. It was of old and strange design, sharp in places, and black and very heavy. He said it was authentic and historical, and could be in a very fine museum indeed.

However it did cause discomfort nonetheless, leaving blue bruises, red welts, and scratches on the skin. I thought: Excuse me. Perhaps it is an honor to be scratched up most historically.

Still I was worried and wished to shelter my arms and legs. Otherwise they would go the way of the foot, and I would be one giant deformity. And quite a burden to others, certainly. After the first incident of history I did not wish to upset Mr. D. But I felt I should probably leave anyway. So I took my towel and my box and sneaked out the door and down the stairs and went stealthily back to the park and the tree.

And there I lay on the wide flat branch and looked up

at the clouds in the blackness, and the halo around the moon. They passed over me as the leaves moved above my head too, in the breeze. And the universe was deep forever, and I knew I was a star among billions.

I was a tiny dull star. But I was in good company.

However Mr. D. found out where I was again, because I was not too crafty. He came there late at night while I was sleeping. And he brought two other larger men who put me in his car and took me back. And thereafter he was prone to lock the door when he left me in the room, with not only one but two keys.

And after that there was quite a bit of history.

Mr. D. would always roll into a ball following history and scrunch his fists up to his face and be ashamed. He would kneel at my feet and say, "You are fine, right? You are fine."

He would say, "This actually did not happen. It was a figment of our imagination. Do you realize that? A figment. Not real. I don't want you to just say it! Don't just say what I tell you to! I want you to know it. It was not real, and it did not happen. Do you know what I mean?"

And he would grip my shoulders when he said this and look at me intently.

And to himself he would say, "I am a good, good man. I am a benefactor. Indeed."

Anyway, I was mostly alone, although Mr. D. brought me many books to read and also records that played

the music of violins and cellos. After he left each time, I
would feel quite relieved, and sit among the dim lamps he
had placed around the room listening to the violins and
cellos. And if I tried, in the cones of light cast by these
lamps, the ceiling was a lake that shivered and the floor
appeared to be a plain with tall grass waving, dotted, on
the distant horizon, with thousands of black dots that
were the ghosts of buffalo.

I saw how every room can be a land, and not all people
choose the rooms they live in.

This would prove useful to me. For sometimes I would
close my eyes and think that I was anywhere.

During the day I stood at the window, which was quite
large but could not be opened, and watched the people
on the street below. And I thought of all the space around
them and how anything could happen; and now or then
I would quickly be overjoyed. I would imagine all the
absent friends moving around in distant countries, and
hear strange music fold the flat line of time into curves
and rushes, bending the air into a quick shiver of an
impulse that swayed, trembled, and soared.

And if this feeling lasted for an instant, I would sit and
think about the instant for hours.

When Mr. D. plied the tool, he was frequently red in the
face, swollen and puffed up. He liked to pretend I was his
wife and then belabor me. "Harlot!" he would grumble, and
chase me around the room. But his real wife was at home in

the house where they lived, or often, when he came to see me, she was playing tennis or having cocktails at the club with, as he said, all the other ladies. He brought a picture of his wife, and it reminded me at once of an eminent person.

I had read about this famous person in one of my books. His name was Winston Churchill.

Mr. D. said he did not have children. His wife had not wished for any when she was young, and then she became too old. And now she could never have them, he said. And he said it quite often.

Sometimes Mr. D. brought a dress of hers or a piece of jewelry, and this I was made to wear before he belabored me. He would ask me to run and drag myself before him, crawling in her dress or skirt or nightgown, and act afraid. Mr. D. tended to be quite satisfied when I whimpered or cried. But then he would go away without saying anything.

After Mr. D. was loud and hard and busy, he would become quiet and turn inside. He would skulk and glance around furtively and be gruff. And he would not admit history. As soon as something was over, it had never happened, according to Mr. D. So that was confusing. History was not history, for Mr. D.

History was only gone.

Also he changed his mind frequently. One day he tended to put her dress on me, or heavy clip-on earrings or pins of hers, which were ovals of brown with the tiny white heads of other ladies on them. And then he would grow frantic, ply the tool, and kick my ribs with the heels of his shoes while I said, "Excuse me!" He would call me his wife's name many times in a row, and it was clear he was trying to forget she was not me. He would call her a stone or a waste or a barren box, and say she was killing him.

And after him, he would say, there would be only nothing. Which was her fault apparently.

But then later he began to say, "Oh my wife, what a fine lady. I would take you to meet her only she is very ill." Or if I asked him why he was so angry, he would become livid and deny everything. "Do not sully her name."

I had to roll on the ground and cover my face sometimes, and rubbed the skin off my kneecaps trying to get away. On hands and knees, I would scrabble across the wooden floor until the pads of my fingers were bristling with splinters. I would hide under the bed while he paced and paced, waiting for me to give up, and I would stare at the splinters. Somehow they bothered me more than the wetness of my back or tenderness of my thighs, which stung when they touched each other.

At night I would lie in bed on my side, as I could not touch my back or my front to the sheets, and worry the splinters with my teeth. This hardly worked. But luckily, by and by the old man brought me a bag of lipsticks and eye shadows, and told me that I should brush the color blue onto my eyelids. And in this slick bag with flowers painted on it I found a pair of tweezers that saved my fingertips.

After a while I grew a little accustomed to the discom-

forts, and the surface of the skin on my back was hard-
ened from old cuts that healed. I learned to bite down on
a stick I had snapped off a rubber plant that stood forlorn,
with yellowing leaves, in the corner of the bathroom.

And later, now that all the years have passed, on occasion I turn my head and look at the scars. And then I feel
like the map of a country, seen from miles up in the stratosphere. The scratches are both indents and outbursts: dry
riverbeds where water once was prone to run, bumps and
tucks in ridges snaking across the skin as mountain ranges
will snake across a continent. And the ones on my back,
from the leather rope with the knots, are blades of grass
bent in the same direction by a strong wind.

So I feel like a planet, both a planet and an insect.
Because when I look at them I also see Mr. D. and his
purple nose and remember crawling. I remember hiding
under the bed, a scurrying brown dinosaur.

Seen from far above, I could be either of them, or then
also nothing.

Presently Mr. D.'s dear ancient wife became deceased.
So all he could do was come into my room and mutter to
himself and weep, his thin shoulders shaking.

Finally, he said we were going to go far away.

So I was allowed to go out of the room finally. I was
allowed to venture down the crowded street, shuffling
along the gravel until we got to the car. The air was fresh,
and I thought I was in the newest place in the world.

The world was so new that it was brightly shining.

Mr. D. nudged my back every time we passed anyone, hissing, "Shh," and then clearing his throat and smiling if anyone looked. Once in the black car we squealed off, raising billows of dust. And the car took us down to the harbor and the glittering water beyond its mouth.

A young man put down a small bridge for us, and we walked from the pier onto a dark blue, shining ship with no sails that belonged to Mr. D.'s company.

The walls were all gone, which was the best thing that had ever happened to me.

There were boats all around, rocking gently, and in the sky there were long planes, and seagulls with knowing eyes strutted on the deck and the pavement nearby.

So then with a grand noise from the engine we left, and the city was behind us.

Of course there were still rules and even a routine. We went from city to city and sometimes to beaches without cities. And when we left each port, the old man would set about me once again with tools and history. And always the new cuts would heal while we were still on the open ocean, before another port would rise above the surface of the sea with towers and its gray halo of air. His wife's name was not mentioned anymore, except once when Mr. D. said she had turned into a saint. Every week he told a florist to send a new wreath to her grave with white roses. And once a week on Sunday he would say grace before we ate, and also say that he wished she was here.

So now I was whoever he told me to be, but the end was the same as before. Mr. D. dearly loved flying into a rage. Although he did so, on the ship, with lesser frequency.

Anyway, I was so glad to be out of my room I hardly minded the history.

There was a small boat with a sail that the crew would sometimes drop off the side for me when there was no land around as far as the eye could see. It was called a Sunfish. On the Sunfish I learned to pull the ropes this way and that, so that the wind would steer the boat and buffet and whip through me. Sometimes I got to stand alone on the Sunfish in the tossing wind that had no aspect but breath, and pillowed arms and fingers everywhere.

When we anchored the big boat in the shallows of a deserted cove, I would wrap layers and layers of torn bands of cloth tightly around my cuts, to keep out the bite of saltwater. And I would swim and dive with stiff motions and float on my back, face turned up to the sky, until I felt the water begin to seep through the cloth or my hands or my feet growing numb.

Finally we landed on a shore where Mr. D. decided we should stay for a while. There were jungles there of tall trees with waxy dark green leaves, and bowl-shaped plants full of water that grew in the crooks of branches and teemed with spiders and tadpoles. In the distance were great black mountains that curved in on the sides but were flat on the top. We lived in a house with a roof made of the bark of spiny trees. And when the rain came, everywhere was pouring silver for weeks, and the black soil ran weaving down the beach and made braids of black and gray across the white sand to the sea. I would walk along the frothy hem of the ocean at low tide and find shrimp the size of lobsters washed up on the sand, in a tangle of seaweed.

I was overwhelmed and made ridiculous with pleasure by this. I thought, If only all of us could have an island, and the sea.

Those days Mr. D. seldom spoke to me, but to a telephone that he preferred. And he seemed to forget about history and let me move around without looking at me.

There were two boys, younger than I was but stronger, living near us in the forest, who would creep up and find me in the hammock and touch the skin between my toes on the lame foot and run away laughing. Once they perched a purple horned beetle there, and it fell down onto my ankle with its legs cycling, and I screamed. But after some days of this they lingered and stared at me, and beckoned one morning. I followed them across a string of mossy rocks over a waterfall and down the side of a ravine full of ferns that grew as high as my waist.

We came to a clearing with huts on stilts, and one of these was their home. I met their family, who lived in a large hut with several other families and did not wear too much clothing. A woman with one milky white eye gave me a yellow piece of fruit to eat, and pulled on my wrist to show me a small infant in the corner that appeared to be newly born. It was a boy with a cord coming out of his stomach and soft, shining brown skin.

Then we left the hut and sat down in the middle of the clearing, and they started to teach me their words. One of them held up a stone and said something, and then I had to repeat it. One of them pointed to his chin and said another word. And I repeated that too. They laughed and pointed at me, but it was not the same sound as the laugh of Mr. D. And then they taught me the word for *brother*.

But I had just learned the word for *elbow*, at least so I think, when there was a sudden shaking of the ground and we looked up and saw dark metal whales crashing down on us from above with rat-tat-tats flashing out the sides of their bellies. One of them loosed a ball of fire that fell crashing into the trees and right away split a hut down the middle so that thatch and black smoke and sparks floated everywhere and made it hard to see. And then there were shattering noises that hurt our ears and all around people running and shrieking and scrambling up the side of the ravine. And we just sat there with our hands over our faces. Then soldiers burst out of the jungle, running with guns from all around and shooting. And they dropped from up high and came down the side of the ravine on bright ropes, and the fleeing people had to turn around again.

I always have followed crowds, because I want to be with them. It may be a deficiency.

Anyway, on this occasion there was nothing to choose. The soldiers herded us out of the clearing, through the forest on the other side of the huts, where I had never been. They gave us orders in French, which I understood a bit from talking to the cook on Mr. D.'s ship. We walked for a long time, with snakes slithering past our feet and cobwebs breaking on our arms and faces as they pushed us through the underbrush with the ends of their guns. And we were afraid and not knowing what would happen. The air was thick and moist. So wetness streaked our faces and ran into our eyes. I wished I knew more words than *stone, chin, hair, elbow, breast,* and *brother.* But we had to be quiet: once a man yelled and a soldier hit him with the rifle and left him lying on the ground, and the woman who had walked beside him sobbed as she kept walking until the sounds coming from her were rough as sandpaper.

I could see freshly cut branches where the soldiers had hacked their way through with big knives ahead of us. And once when I was panting from the exhaustion of walking, my mouth hung open and the next thing I knew there was a fat, furry body on my tongue, nearly filling my mouth. I could not breathe but choked and spit it out, and when it dropped and scuttled away I saw it was a large spider. I was coughing and would have let out a loud sound if one of the boys from the village had not quickly touched my lips to keep me quiet.

And then when the sun was going down we were joined by a group of others, also with guns and knives to their backs, glassy-eyed and stumbling before some more soldiers, who talked loudly and shouted and seemed to joke as though it was a game. "Faut pas tuer, il a dit," said one of them, when another put his gun playfully into a younger man's ear. I knew from the cook that *tuer* was what he did to the lobster.

When we came out of the forest, suddenly it was a different kind of island. It was flat and still sandy, but this sand was the color of dried mustard, not the white sand that I knew from the beach. There were gray tanks parked in rows with thin cannons on top, and long flat tents and a stretch of concrete runway where small airplanes could land, and jeeps and soldiers rushing everywhere. The black mountains were much closer, looming over us. The air was swarming with helicopters, and some of us, who had never seen machines before that day, began to cry and whimper. Now and then the earth vibrated, and there was a distant boom.

Then they made us all enter a flat house of sticks, with no roof and a floor of wet mud, one door, and one window with bars. No one was permitted to leave. The soldiers locked the door and stood outside it, talking and smoking. Night came on with its distant booms and stars, and we all were so tired from the walking that we fell asleep twisted over each other, our heads on others' stomachs or backs and our cheeks against the mud.

The two young boys who had taught me the words lay next to me, one of them rolled into a ball, on his side. And while he was sleeping he sighed and nudged closer to me, and I put my arms around him. And the mud grew warm beneath my cheek.

And in the early hours when dawn was coming and a light spread out and seeped between the sticks, we heard a wailing rise above us and float thinly and sad in the humidity. And some handfuls of food were dropped over the walls, and people crawled and ate the food that lay between us in the mud. It was clumps of rice, which fell apart when they were touched and resembled white worms.

Then the sun rose until it was straight over our heads, and the buzzing flies were all around our ears and in the corners of our eyes. It grew hot and we were thirsty. And then the time came when no one spoke anymore, not even in whispers. Some soldiers came through the crowd now and then, cawing like crows and laughing. They chewed at crusts of bread and tore at fruit between their teeth, and flung the crumbs and the rinds and peels of fruit among us, where they lay. Some of us finally ate the rinds and peels, while others turned their faces away.

And so time passed like this, various days and nights. To forget the hollowness and the thirst, sometimes we dozed listlessly. And then the flies left and mosquitoes came, for it was dusk again, and in the sky above us were bands of pink and gray.

Presently I was exhausted from the heat and being thirsty, and being awake was like sleeping and dreaming. And then there came a small amount of men in a van, and some of them wore suits and carried guns, and were white in the face like me. They swarmed around, and then a new, smaller helicopter was rising above the crowds, the floor dipping away and then again jolting, and in it was me. And Mr. D., swearing.

Pod

When we first flew off the island and were put down on the ship, and the helicopter rose and whirred away to the horizon till it was only a fly again, a strange gray snow was falling around us. Its flakes were landing everywhere, drifting and smearing. And through the haze I could see that one of the black mountains on the horizon seemed to be jetting out steam, smoking like a chimney. It was filling the sky above itself with clouds.

I asked Mr. D. about it, saying, "Is it a volcano?"

Mr. D. clenched his teeth very tightly. He said, "Forget it. There's no volcano there, okay?"

I said, "But how about the others? Will it hurt them?"

But Mr. D. was very angry at me. He was so angry he could hardly speak. He said, What if I got him killed, little bitch. And he set upon me mightily.

So I fell over and caved in. I slept forever, awash in history.

Certainly Mr. D. did not know his own strength.

Still, when I woke up, a few days out on the sea apparently, the sun was not hard or bright anymore: there were shadows. Out the porthole beside my bed I could see a clean blue sky and towers of cloud, bulging like cotton, over a quiet green ocean.

I looked at myself also and saw that some of the blood that had dripped down my legs from the new cuts had dried into a red-brown powder. So in the warm daze of first being awake I thought I was a good old machine on the farm, which rusted but still plowed on doggedly. And I felt relieved and satisfied still to be functioning.

And then I stumbled onto the deck and felt the soft winds like pillows blow against the raw parts of my skin.

And when Mr. D. saw me, he was sheepish and looked at me a new way, which was almost polite.

The months that we passed above the water after this were a cocoon. The sea was always softly moving beneath us; we floated in a bubble, gently. For me there was only one thing occurring, and no intrusions.

It turned out I was having a baby.

Mr. D. brought a woman aboard the ship, who wore a stiff white dress and white shoes with heels like steady slopes. She was the caretaker, a nurse, he said. For the child and, he said winking, for me. She knew all about infants, their care and feeding.

But when he introduced us the nurse kept staring at me.

Then she said, "My God!"

Mr. D. did not know what she meant at first, I could tell. But he recovered quickly.

"The rebels," he said. "It looks worse than it is."

She turned to him with her mouth hanging open and then bustled me away.

Later, after she had smoothed clear ointment and taped gauze pads on the cuts and given me several shots, she went and spoke to Mr. D. behind a door. Their voices were low. When they were finished speaking, she came out with a serious face. And briefly I thought she had learned something true and was lifted.

But then she said, "You poor thing!" and patted me neatly on the head.

After that the nurse occasionally spoke to me of what she called my tribulations. She did not do so easily, but rather tiptoed up to me whispering she knew it must be very painful. However, I could tell that she secretly wished to hear all the details of the history. Or even see a movie. For now and then while she was dressing an injury she would shake her head and say, "So, this one—how did this happen?"

And I would gaze absently at the chair in the corner with sailboats and tillers on the upholstery, where, if you looked closely at the backs of the wooden legs a few inches from the floor, you would be able to see thin, deep lines etched horizontally. These were the places where wires had rubbed and dug into the wood while they were looped around my ankles.

But no one would look.

Rather, she would say quickly, "I mean Christ. Haven't they heard of the Geneva Convention?"

And at last, when I knew what she was saying to me, I told her, "But the people on the island did not harm me."

However she thought I was confusing what had actually been with what I wanted to be, because I was so weak. She was convinced I did not know what a fact was.

And to this day I have to agree.

Mr. D. was kind to me those days, bringing me water now and then, or other cool drinks, and grudgingly speaking to me. He was also polite and would watch me carefully as I walked past him fatly.

So for all that time, when Mr. D. was prone to bring me a glass of water with a slice of lemon, and the caretaker nurse was always seeing if I was feeling well, I was on a home ship, the ship of home. The sea was wide around, but we were floating. There was no history, no tools at all, and there was nothing to wish for.

I think now that it must have been paradise, where a person sheds their limbs, molting, forgetting discomfort, and dropping their body. In that place hardly anything happens, and even the future is gone.

There was the rocking of the boat, and the sun was lazy.

However, in the end this part of my life would become a moth and fly away from me. For always people fly, and all remembrance flies into the sun as it sets, changing shape in the dark. The details of the months and years fly too, and everything is prone to fly away and disappear.

And I am left.

The day Brother was born, the nurse gave me shots from a needle as long as half of my arm. I remember the bed, and Mr. D. coughing.

When I woke up I was alone and aching. I got up and went to look, full of panic. And I found them in a supply room, where a large quiet fan moved the air.

The room had held cans of tomato and bean soup and bottles of juice previously. Now however the shelves were gone and it was painted pale blue. The old man and the nurse were standing beside a wooden crib, leaning close over the infant. And I saw right away that Mr. D.'s face was not the same as it had been before. There were curtains of pride hanging from his eyelids as he bent his head.

Above them a mobile turned in the breeze from the fan, and paper seagulls fluttered.

I went over and pushed myself between them, and that was the first time I saw him.

I picked him up and could not believe it. I thought to myself: he flew out of a volcano.

A volcano that never existed.

And right then I called him the word for *brother,* since *stone, elbow, chin, hair,* or *breast* would not do.

After a minute of me standing there still, giddy and blinking at Brother with my face very close to his, Mr. D. interrupted. He tapped me on the shoulder and nodded to the nurse. "She is the boss," he said sternly.

So Mr. D. or the nurse often followed me around the ship when I was carrying Brother. Which was mostly.

Because I have been sure of one thing in my life: and that was Brother. He did not speak yet but in other ways he was clear to me. He played jokes, such as to lie on his back like a tipped-over beetle, waving and peddling his limbs in the air. After a while his round gaze began to follow me closely, and there were private secrets between us that we kept without saying a single word.

Brother and I had a code.

So I stuck to him like glue, and only left him alone to go to sleep. Even then, sometimes I would curl up on a chair next to him.

It is hard to say what Brother ever made of me, but I made a galaxy out of him. And all the lonely stars spiraled toward the center, glowing.

The ship went from harbor to harbor and up and down coasts. We would have a few hours in each city, always with Mr. D. walking behind us, stopping often to make his business calls, and the nurse or one of the crewmen watching us closely. I liked to walk with Brother hanging in a cushioned pack on the front of me, along the docks and rails that presided over the edges of the land. We walked along boardwalks and beaches with trees, and I was pleased to have the solid ground beneath us.

I took each step cautiously at first, peering over the top of Brother's soft pate, but his head would bounce anyway. His neck seemed rubbery, and he did not care too much about keeping it stiff. And he stared up at my chin all the time with soft blue eyes.

Here and there I sat with Brother in gardens, or I would wade with him through shallow waters in an inlet, with trailing and slimy plants around my calves sometimes, seaweed brushing on the surface of me. And I would hold him there above the water and all three of us were there, the ocean, him, and me.

Some afternoons we watched the rolling of the tides before the purple and the yellow dusk leaked from the sky. We sat in places paved with cobblestones, where birds would alight in flocks of gray and brown to peck at crusts. We saw people pass us in those foreign lands and go about their business there, or in the slow heat in a market, where striped cloths shivered in the wind and cinnamon and cloves and cardamom were fragrant in the air. I thought, What if we could join them one day?

I dreamed of impossible escapes, made fluidly. Brother and I would put on a deep-sea diving suit. It would have a hump on the back for him to sit in, and two helmets, one large and one small. Late at night while the ship was docked we would creep through a great silver duct in its belly. We would cut a hole in the hull of the ship with a diamond saw and slip into the sea like a slick fish. With bubbles weaving and winding up behind us we would make a deep arc through the water, rising to emerge on a strip of hilly land covered in small houses with tangled gardens, lit orange inside and full of nice families, and watched over by a lighthouse's warm beacon.

And inside the lighthouse we would drink hot drinks and dry ourselves by a fire.

And so Brother would be free.

However, the old man always kept us in his field of view. He had begun to dote on Brother and wanted to give him his last name, he told me. Once I stood outside the door to the nursery and heard him telling the nurse that Brother would grow up to run his business. He said, "This little guy will oversee a thousand mines in the next century. You watch me."

I thought then that Brother had changed him, because he did not practice history. But later I did not know if he had changed. Since he had Brother, he did not need another way to leave himself behind. So he did not have to make his mark on me.

But he may have been envious of Brother and me.

Because soon enough a day came when he said we would stay on dry land for the night. We were dropping off the nurse in a famous city, and from there she would fly home. Mr. D. said that from then on I could take care of Brother myself, since I had learned. So I was happy.

We said good-bye to the nurse at the airport, where we had driven with her in a long black car. We watched her airplane taxi down the runway and take off into the sky, which I had not seen before. And I held Brother up.

Then we took him to a restaurant and sat him in a high chair. He was always quiet: he stared around the table and then fastened his eyes on me. We liked to have staring contests.

Mr. D. hardly spoke to us that evening but stayed on a telephone they brought him on a plate.

Later, when I put Brother to sleep in our large hotel room in a cot with rails beside me, I recall he held my finger insistently. But I was feeling dizzy, and not too well, and fell back onto my bed.

And the next day I did not wake up until it was afternoon. My head throbbed and it was dark in the room, because the blinds were pulled down.

I got out of bed and saw that Mr. D.'s bed was empty. He was not there anymore. And neither was Brother.

I opened the blinds: outside the window the sun had risen quite high, but the light was flat and gray. At first I was confused, though not alarmed; but soon I was running around. I flapped my arms like a chicken's wings and squawked and squealed.

After a while, when I calmed down, I found that in the room with me were a number of small possessions I had gained over the years, as well as some documents. There was everything there I had kept on the ship. The closets were hung with my clothes, every garment I owned, which was not too many. And on the chest of drawers beside me there were some stacks of paper money, neatly lined up against the wall.

On the table was a vase of dried flowers, and hollow pods that looked like wood, with empty round holes in them where seeds must have once been.

But still, for all these things the room was a vacuum.

I ran out of the room and down the street and farther and farther, lost and found and lost again till I reached the harbor. But the ship I knew was gone. It had vanished utterly.

Always I thought that I would know Brother, regardless of the years that passed. But like the ocean he would not know me.

3

The sounds of leaving were scrapes, rumbles, and the rolling of small rubber balls along the floors, building up and fading. I had become used to this last noise because the orderlies had always brought us our meals on tall, rectangular metal carts stacked from the floor up with trays. After my last bowl of oatmeal, when the noises began, I said to myself: They are moving the furniture first. And then they will move other things, such as patients.

I did not doubt it.

At that time it did not occur to me to pound against my door brashly. I said to myself, Everyone is busy. I said, One day soon they will come for me.

So I sat on the side of my bed dressed as best I could be, that is, with my blue robe neatly tied at the back and wearing a pair of small paper boots with their cuffs in scallops from the elastic. These a nurse had once given to me before she touched my temples with cotton, spreading a see-through jelly. I was waiting.

I held this pose on the bed for many hours with my hands clasped in my lap as large objects were trundled down the corridor outside, rattling furiously. I did not know what they were of course—maybe machines with blips and tubes—but at that time I chose to picture wheelbarrows lined with goblets trembling rim against rim, and carriages strung with bells and hammers.

Of course I knew there were no musical instruments in the building, except for a child's xylophone that was kept in the rec room, where I used to go to read books. It had convex metal plates each a color of the rainbow, which someone had decided was the correct instrument for insane people, apparently. And certainly it had seemed to be an instrument that only an insane person would wish to master.

I was trying to be patient in my waiting, but in fact the excitement rose in me through the rib cage, past the lungs, and into the throat. I was seized by the knowledge that I was going to leave the building at long last. And even if it was only for transport to another place like this one, it was still worth the anticipation.

I planned the sights I felt I was guaranteed: bushes and trees and the wind moving them, dome of the sky with clouds and rays of sun, a distant horizon. I hoped to leave at the end of the day, so I could count among these elements the moon and possibly bright Venus rising. I crossed my fingers for that.

Presently the rattles and churning wheels, shouts and

muffled crashes grew few and far between. Still I sat there, believing my wish had been granted and I was going to see the night sky. I would crane my neck out the window of a bus and gaze up into the stratosphere.

But then the sounds died away completely. I abandoned my post on the bed, walked up to my locked door, and knocked on it tentatively. I called out, "Excuse me?"

There was no answer.

Still I did not draw any conclusions. I made myself go to sleep, disappointed but in readiness for a move the next day.

Which did not occur, needless to say. There were never any more voices or sounds, except for what I think was a pigeon or a dove flapping against the eaves somewhere above me, through the heaviness of the ceiling.

Hair

It began to grow in gray just a few weeks after Brother was lost, pale strands glinting. And it was white all the way from the roots to the ends before I was even twenty. I had heard of such incidents occurring, such as when ghosts were seen, but was still surprised when I saw it had happened to me.

The foot that healed itself inside the cast, the scalp that instructed my hair to turn white, these parts still confound me.

However, I failed to notice the white hairs for some time. For in the weeks after Brother was taken I did not brush my hair, eat, wash, or dress and undress with regularity. So I am sure I was unpleasant for scrutiny. I would find myself waking up late at night with a torn piece of bread and honey on my chest, a saucer and empty glass lying alongside my knee. Or I would run to the bathroom and turn on the shower nozzles full force because the room service man had looked quite disapproving of me.

But then I would forget that I had done so and leave the taps running until a blocked pipe beneath the floor burst and there was a flood. I found out soon that the ceiling of the room beneath me had darkened and sagged and rained plaster in jagged fragments; and it fell down on several naked gentlemen. I apologized profusely.

Myself I noticed nothing about me. Everything I had was turned toward the rest of the world.

I had gone to the men at the desk in the hotel and asked them, begging, if they knew anything about Mr. D., where he had gone or what his plans might be. I tried to give them all the stacks of money if they would only tell me. But shaking their heads, they said they had no information. And they were very sorry. So then I asked them what to do about a missing person and they said go to the police, so I did.

I told the policemen about history, not at length but briefly. They said it was unfortunate. Then I told them about Brother disappearing and Mr. D. leaving stacks of money, but they only shrugged and said there were no laws on the books that would prove useful to me. So they could not help. It was not their jurisdiction.

In fact, one of them said, it was no one's jurisdiction except Jesus Christ's.

However, I was too crafty for that and said, "But he is dead I believe."

Moreover with no visible means of support, as they put it, a lame foot, and being barely the age of majority, I was hardly a fit parent as far as they could see.

So that was all of the kindness of the state. I knew that a child was not a possession. I never believed that Brother belonged to me. I only believed he *was* me.

And I knew what Mr. D. had practiced on me and that he was not prone to charity. Because the tools from past centuries, and the wires and the knives, might have been all right for me but they could not be plied on Brother. For Brother there could be no history. I pleaded with the air and said, Give me ten years with Brother and take away all the rest. Or I said, give me five years, or one.

Or just one day to rescue him, and then vanish me.

I was trying to make bargains with every invisible force that could be.

I knew that I had hurt Brother myself, and it was all my fault. Because Mr. D. would always be Mr. D. Which I knew, certainly. Yet I had never crawled out through a silver duct with Brother on my back and a diamond saw in my hand. I had never pumped us out with the bilge, thin as straws, or made a break across the open ocean in the Sunfish.

I had never run flailing and screaming through the open, where others could see, clutching Brother, leaving behind me Mr. D.

True, Mr. D. would have found and punished me finally, but still I could have left Brother in one of those glowing homes beneath the lighthouse, full of nice families.

But instead he was with a person who did not know his own strength.

I have known many in my life. They are as abundant as the princes with gold teeth.

At night I could not fall asleep for biting at my fingers, so they became ragged. I attacked the ends of my person until they weakened and frayed, fingertips, feet, and the hair on my head.

When I lapsed into sleep I was chided by thoughts of Brother grown old suddenly, rising in a steel dragonfly over a dying country. Twisted into a hard dry knot, he had become a soldier. Or he had become a locust the size of a man. He was eyeless like a worm, cut into a thousand pieces and all of them moving in the mustard-colored sand restlessly.

I had no destination, certainly, and for a long time I kept hoping they might come back to the room and to me, Mr. D. suddenly relenting and coming with his face wreathed in apologies. So I stayed at the hotel every night and searched during the day.

It would appear that waiting has not served me well over the years, for they never returned.

I went back to the port several times, looking for the harbormaster. Finally I saw one of his assistants sitting in the office. So I knocked on the open door and asked him if he could trace Mr. D.'s ship by the nameplate on the bow, which read *Ice Queen of Miami*. I think he took pity on me because he said possibly. And told me to come back tomorrow.

So I did. He had made inquiries over the radio and then even by telephone. He said yes, the ship recently left her mooring. So you are right; she is not here anymore.

But sadly, he said, she is nowhere else either.

I asked him how that could be. And he said if she did not want to be found, she had probably changed her name and her number as well, so that her movements could not be followed. It was possible, he said, to buy false papers for a ship.

So I trudged away. And I telephoned Mr. D.'s business, where he always had a secretary. And I asked to speak to her. I told her who I was, and she said she had never heard of me. So I told her I had been on the ship and heard her voice before, coming out of a box when Mr. D. dictated letters or gave her instructions. It sounded like a bark. But she said that this had never happened. Yes Mr. D. was the CEO of the company, she said. But he worked out of the home or the office chiefly. As far as she knew he had never set foot on a boat in his life. He preferred golf to sailing. And anyway, years ago the company had sold the power yacht it once owned.

No it was not called Ice Queen of Miami.

I said, "But I lived on that ship with him for years, several years we lived on the Ice Queen until a few days ago."

She said I was not in charge of certain faculties, and then hung up the phone.

The next morning I began to comb all of the hotels in the famous city, four or five in a day, asking for Mr. D. When the clerks told me, as they tended to immediately, that there was no one of that name registered here, I thanked them, nodded, and sat down on a flowery sofa or in a chair. Then I waited in the lobby for three hours precisely.

I did this in case he was pretending to be someone else.

I was very alert in my research, perhaps overly so. Because I suspected Mr. D. might be traveling in disguise, I tended to skulk. I skulked and I lurked. I would read a newspaper or a magazine from the coffee table and focus my eyes over the top like an obvious detective. And then when a guest made his way across the lobby, my gaze would follow him. I concentrated on persons who wore a means of distraction, such as hats with wide brims, high collars and beards, prominent glasses with heavy frames, or bushy wigs.

Once I caught sight of a woman with a red scarf over her head, a stomach thick as the trunk of an oak tree, and ankles wider than her feet. Just as she reached the elevator she turned and glanced at me, and I saw with a shock that her nose had blossomed into a purple flower.

I knew right away that the bulk of her person could easily conceal Mr. D., wrapped in pillows and stuffing and then covered up with her ruffled and bulging clothing. So I ran across the lobby and threw myself at her feet, promptly.

I said, "Where is he? Please I will do anything."

But she beat on me with her purse. And soon the hotel employees carried me out onto the sidewalk. One advised me to seek counseling.

Instead I moved into a humbler hotel, where the bathroom with its cold tile floor was down the hall and beside my slim bed there was a gas heater that asked for coins. Under my feet in the morning when I rose from the slumping bed was a worn brown carpet. And I would look out the window and see a rooftop of pigeons.

More and more it seemed I was in the city without a reason.

So eventually I left. It was all I could do.

But I made up my mind to go up and down coasts and ask at every port if they had seen the Ice Queen of Miami. I did not expect them to say yes, but still I wanted to ask. I wanted to do all I could to find Brother. Because I thought it was possible, although very faintly, that if I never gave up I would be forgiven.

Whenever I opened the shoebox and pulled out a sheaf of banknotes to buy passage on a ferry or warm soup in winter, my fingers felt sticky and I would recall dried flowers, dull orange in a vase, and the empty hotel room full of flat gray light. So I did not touch the money often but worked alongside the road, between buses or train stations where there were farms. I would ride in the cars of strangers until I saw a fruit stand, and then ask for work there.

I picked grapes, peaches, and nectarines and carried bundles along dirt roads. Once I folded the tops of boxes in a shed where they packed apples, and another time I helped to put together handles and rubber skipping ropes. I walked up and down beaches selling ice cream and frozen fruit on sticks to prone individuals whose skin was gleaming brown. And I spent the nights in barns and garages, or on beaches and in orchards in summer and spring. I had a one-person tent shaped not unlike a coffin.

I knew what coffins looked like because one night, in a small town on the mouth of a river where I arrived in a bus late and cold, the streets were all dark and silent and the restaurants and stores were all closed, except for one, which was very brightly lit. And in the store there were coffins of all shapes and sizes, some of them even red or pink or white and decorated with painted flowers, and the size of babies. I stood and stared, but there was no one there. But the store was open to the street.

So seasons passed in which I felt the space around me that Brother had left. My arms tended to hang idle beside me, and I seldom knew what to do with them. Disbelief flowed over me for months and years. Late at night I would sit up on my blanket and whisper to my campfire or the back of a toolshed: None of it ever happened. There is no such thing.

I felt his absence for longer than I had known him.

But I was coming to see that there are no impossibilities, that what seems impossible is only perched on the rim of the mind, teetering. And then sometimes it tips closer and falls in and is possible, either for the first time or again.

And it was true that I went many places.

I walked down between high arched rows of pecan trees and over grassy dunes filled with small scuttling crabs and the hushing sound of the tide. And I found myself in raw places too, the sprawling cities backed up against the oceans. I saw that people in these places, which were infested by plagues of buildings, could not say where their distress came from, and thought it was a mystery. Many had never seen land without roads and thought all views were like their own, nothing but wide and intertwining highways covered in angry, glittering cars, and brown and gray concrete fields. There were flat hard surfaces where the forests and the rivers and swamps used to be, and over them the dirt of living washed into the seas.

But even though I went far, in those years, I went nowhere at all. Except toward Brother, wanting. Desire was a straight line for me, and the roadsides fell away on each side of me, into nothing.

Now when I consider it, I know I could not have done it differently. But still I long and I wish for the sights and the smells, and for the people I missed, that were all around me.

I never looked for Brother directly, but still I hoped I might catch sight of him in a stroller crossing a street, or his low shadow in a window, reflected dimly.

And Brother never grew old for me.

It was fall, in one of the rare years when a comet streaked overhead, when I recognized my stupidity. I was standing in a small library in a fishing town in the country of Brazil. And I turned from a rack of magazines and looked down at a large, flat book spread open on a wooden lectern, with yellowing pages. It was called *Atlas of the World* and was in English. And the page it was open to showed all the continents. And the oceans in between, marked ATLANTIC and PACIFIC.

I had seen globes before, but I had never been told that the blue parts were oceans and the green ones were land. When I looked at the ocean it was seldom blue, and the land was not green either, often.

And so I never had known how much of the world was ocean.

And how much coast.

Presently I met a kind woman who let me paint her shutters, and also clean the floors and walls of her house for several days. She brought me salads made with the hearts of palm and olive oil, and afterward she offered me a pudding to eat. She gave me many desserts but always called them puddings. She also taught me to speak a few words of her language, which was Portuguese.

So one evening I sat with her on the front porch of her small wooden house. And I watched others pass us in the street as she did many sums, plying a pen on a piece of newspaper. Every so often she would consult a small version of the *Atlas of the World* open beside her on the steps. She added and added until she had long winding towers of numbers.

And these sums, she told me when she was finished with the adding, showed that if I kept going as fast as I could along the coastlines of the world, I would have covered most of them by the year 2093. Not counting, she said, Greenland or the North or South Pole.

I thanked her and washed the dishes in her sink and then took a walk through the village as it grew dark. People were laughing, dancing, and drinking intoxicants outside restaurants on the hilly cobblestone streets, and many old churches were strung with lights.

I was at a loss. I did not know how to complete my apology.

And I had spent all the years wandering in case I saw Brother, but it had come to nothing.

So I walked around the city watching people dance until a clock on a belltower read four in the morning. And it was when I passed a broken-down cemetery on a corner that I saw what I could do.

I could make a pilgrimage.

Pencils

When I got back to the city where Mr. D. had found me, it was no longer there.

Excuse me: there was a city of the same name, but the city I knew was gone. Bare avenues with blank, square buildings stretched where there had once been narrow curved roads shaded by old trees. Even the park was gone, and the bronze man that used to stand at its center.

This man had been extremely large and strict. He had a handlebar mustache, rode upon a rearing horse of bronze, and stiffly held up his sword in a challenging fashion. But where the bronze man had sat on his horse with his sword raised was a long-term parking structure with four stories.

I thought sadly: Poor father, your sword was not so sharp after all.

Anyway the streets and buildings were transformed, and there was nothing that I knew. And while I had never wished to leave my traces on the world, yet I always assumed it left its imprints on me. I thought I was at least a place where memories reposed. But here it seemed that I had fished my memories from one great dark whirlpool surrounded by banks of sliding sand, whose pull was always shifting.

And swiftly all the time I had known was a figment, much like me. I was nothing without memory. And I felt dizzy and fell down, with everything disappearing.

• • •

Presently I woke up again on the ground. There was mud clotted in my hair and in the wrinkles of my knuckles.

I gathered up my things and walked until I found a bright yellow sign heralding vacancies. And the next morning I went straight to the lobby downstairs, businesslike, and located a telephone book and began to call cemeteries to find Mrs. D. And I found out there were two persons with her name who had died in one year.

So I went to both graves in both cemeteries, situated on far-distant reaches of the city, east and southwest. I looked at the words engraved on the stones, and I read the dates of birth as well as death.

And these numbers were not too confusing, for one of the two had died at the age of fifty-nine, and the other at age three.

Before I left the hotel, I looked at the calendar on the wall, which showed a bear standing on its hind legs and wearing a frilly bonnet. It said it was a Monday.

I took my tent and a box of nuts and a jug of water, and that night and many nights afterward I slept in a copse of firs on the other side of the cemetery's fence, with a view of the stone. I was only a few feet from a ditch beside the road, but because of the trees and the thickness of their needles no one could see me.

When it rained at night and I was in my tent, the rain made such a patter that I felt as comforted as if I had a home.

The florists' vans came early every morning. There were several of them. I was surprised to learn so many of the dead were in dire need of flowers.

All these vans grew familiar to me, in particular one with two hearts on the side and another with fancy script, long tendrils of plants trailing out of the *Y*s and *P*s and ending in pointed leaves. They often left plastic arrangements in vases that could not be broken. They would go to a grave and take the old plastic flowers away and replace them with new ones in different hues and with different ribbons. So IN MEMORY would turn overnight to THINKING OF YOU.

Finally, while I was wandering among the headstones a caretaker with garden shears spoke to me, asking why I was there. I was silent for a second, hesitating. But then he said, "Is it for the rubbings?" So eagerly I said yes. I did not know what he meant, but as luck would have it soon I would see. He pointed to a grave across the lot where a man was bent over. And he said, "So is he."

I strolled over casually and saw the man was tracing the engraved words *mourned by all* from a stone. He held a piece of paper against the stone and drew over its surface with charcoal until he had covered the sheet with gray lines and the words stood out white. Then he took another slip of paper and traced *who knew her.*

The purpose of this activity was unclear to me, but I did not want to have to leave the graveyard due to being a liar. So I was determined to pursue it as I had said I would. I asked him, "Excuse me. Would you allow me to buy a piece of that charcoal from you?"

He did not have any more sticks of charcoal, only round black nubs he could barely even hold, which he showed me. Instead he gave me several sharpened orange pencils with erasers on their ends. And he said they were almost as good. But he was very generous and would not accept money.

As a result of his generosity I was able to trace a number of gravestones, drawing each tracing out for as long as I could. The caretaker would amble by and look over my shoulder and speak to me kindly, saying for instance, "Oh hmm, that one looks very good."

But I was not skilled, in fact I was clumsy. The cherubs with feathery wings became bees. And in my tent I was amassing a pile of pages bearing faint words such as *taken from us and gathered under God's wing* and *he lived long and simply.*

I had also traced all the words on Mrs. D.'s grave, which said only her name and the dates and *She walked in beauty.*

But it was Monday again soon enough, and no one had left flowers on the grave of Mrs. D. I grew despondent, afraid that Mr. D. had forgotten her finally. And I gave up the tracings and hid myself in the tent for several days, lying on my front and gazing out from between the door flaps.

When a woman with a gray ponytail finally hung the wreath of white roses over Mrs. D.'s stone, it was in the pouring rain on a Sunday. So the cemetery was deserted, a bog of standing water. I was on the other side of the fence huddled in my wet tent gazing out. I was concentrating on not clenching my teeth and not shivering and had my blanket wrapped around me.

I looked up just in time not to miss her.

She wore rubber boots and carried a green umbrella, a wreath, and a spray of eucalyptus. She walked quickly in the direction of Mrs. D.'s grave and once there performed her duty rapidly, placing the wreath so it hung over Mrs. D.'s name. Then she strode to another grave, where she laid down the eucalyptus branch on the grass. And she turned to leave.

So then I ran with my blanket still wrapped around me. I ran and I ran with my feet sinking and slipping in the mud until I came up behind her, but when she turned and saw me coming she also began to run.

I think the blanket looked like a cloak and a hood, and I was very wet and possibly quite dirty. And because of this she became very frightened of me.

As I ran, I called to her not to worry, saying, "Excuse me, excuse me, excuse me!"

But she only said, "Get away from me! Get away!"

And then we were at the curb, and she was unlocking the door of her van. I slowed down, and I walked up behind her asking if she could tell me the whereabouts of Mr. D., but unfortunately she was still alarmed and screeching. I tried to talk to her as she climbed into the van but she slammed the door behind her and locked it quite frantically. Suddenly there was a car behind me, with policemen getting out of it and running up to me.

And I turned around to explain what I was wishing to ask her, but they came and grabbed my arms and put me in the car with them.

Dollar

The sentence was not too long, and I was called a first-time offender. Because, I think, the judge was quite certain I would do additional felonies.

As it turned out I was guilty of an assault even if I did not touch anyone. This was confusing to me. But I was very sorry anyway that I had been so frightening. And I knew I must have made a terrible mistake somehow, in the manner of my running.

Also, the policemen were under the impression for a time that Mr. D.'s dollar bills, which were in my shoebox inside the knapsack I was carrying, had been taken by me unlawfully and without permission from some other person. Or possibly a bank. But then they gave the money back finally, muttering something about the digits printed on it.

After the shower and the powder that was shaken over me, I gave up my bundle of possessions to the woman at the desk and then was led down a hallway. Its walls were close and seemed to have been washed in blue solutions of uncommon purity, which smelled very strong so that my eyes became teary. And the floor too had been steeped in blue solutions, so that I could not help but breathe them in. As my eyes watered I held my breath. Then I stepped through a loud buzzing door, and until I stepped out several months later I was subject again to the kindness of the state. This kindness was a good deal more insistent than others I had known previously.

While I was in my cell, I often lay on my bunk and ran my fingers over the wall beside me. It was scratched and ragged, with seams and lines in the plaster. And while I ran my finger over it I tended to hear the calls back and forth from cell to cell, and inmates bargaining. They were always making deals and exchanges so that, bit by bit, they could acquire more things and widen the circle of their influence. They were trying to build comfort around them like sandbags. But the floodwaters always kept rising.

When we were taken out into the yard no one talked to me at first because I had nothing to offer. Such as cigarettes or tiny pills or special shipments. But after a while some inmates began to ask me to take messages to other inmates while we were having fresh air. One of them who was named Ann-Marie said she liked to watch me limping and trailing my foot across the cement with a message to deliver. She said it was good to have something to rely on, and for her this was the sight of me. She called me Little Dog. Because she said I was small and faithful. So the others called me Little Dog as well.

It made me think of Oscar and Oscar Too.

The messages that I carried were often in strange codes I did not understand, but anyway I was glad to be of service. And when the women with the messages heard I was leaving they all smiled and patted me on the head and shoulder.

The night after I was released I slept on a bench with my shoebox and my knapsack on the ground beneath me. It was warm, and I had walked around all day staring at the elements of the world. Every now and then I would become thrilled and have to run until I was panting. And then stop running and walk again. I felt that the air was delicious, the time and the place were delicious specifically. Now I think anyplace outside would have seemed as delicious to me. I have always wished the present to resemble memory: because the present can be flat at times, and bald as a road. But memory is never like that. It makes hills of feeling in collapsed hours, a scene of enclosure made all precious by its frame.

And when I got out of jail that was how the day was. Instead of remembering my life happily, I was in the middle of it. And I wanted to be held there forever.

Finally in a daze I lay down. I curled up on a wooden bench to sleep, and even the discomfort of the slats did not prevent me.

But when I woke up the next morning my knapsack with the one-man tent was gone, and so were the packets of paper money. They had vanished. It was not surprising, I reflected. Because I had always been careless with the bills that Mr. D. had left me, careless in keeping them. I was sickened by their feel, the grain of them that always seemed slick on the pads of my fingers. I tended to forget that other people would not be as sickened as I was. I forgot that for them the bills did not have the texture of the empty room and of the flat gray light.

Because I had never liked to touch those bills, often I had relied upon people in stores, in their wisdom, to reach into the box themselves and take the amount they needed.

But now there was only a corner of a bill left, old and wrinkled, a torn triangle with a zero on it.

And I found I was able to touch it without displeasure. It was old and useless and could not be spent. What is new is only new once, and then is old and remains old for all time. I feel a tenderness for anything old, because it suffers from not being new.

As for being new myself, when I was I did not even know it.

Anyway, after that I had to proceed differently, mainly to look for things in garbage cans and dumps instead of buying them. And warmth and dryness were not always assured anymore.

But I had not forgotten, still, about finding Mr. D.

So I went to the building where he had kept me before we sailed on the sea. And I did not find him, but I read the name of a real estate company that was written above the mailboxes in the small lobby. And I went to its address.

The woman who worked at the desk, who sported very large hair and was painting her fingernails with glittery purple stuff, said the company had not owned the building back in the olden days when I used to live there. And she looked in a file and found the name of the old landlord, even handing me his address.

However, when I went to visit him a young woman with a droopy face opened the door.

"You mean my father," she said, and nodded. "He had emphysema."

She let me into her home and offered me a cup of tea and a cookie while sitting bent over on the edge of her seat and plucking at the skirt that lay over her knees. The fabric was bumpy. I was glad that I had washed my own clothing, which was a pair of overalls I would be wearing for approximately two years. I looked around at the profusion of plants on shelves and windowsills, and she told me about her father. He was from Hungary. He smoked three packs of cigarettes every day without any filters. And then he died.

But when he was alive he had owned two apartment buildings. "They were mortgaged to the hilt," she said with a note of apology. This seemed dangerous to me so I nodded in sympathy.

I explained to her what I was looking for. She was extremely kind and said what I needed was the lease. I could look through the boxes of records in her closet if I wanted to. She thought they went back fifteen years, but she had not looked at them since before the funeral.

So I sat down and went through them carefully. It was difficult. Because they were not in order and who knew where Mr. D.'s rental agreement might be. That night I went out of her house as though I had a home, slept on the bench as usual, washed in the bathroom of a library, and returned the next day as she had invited me to.

When I found the lease after three days of looking, however, it did not contain Mr. D.'s name but only that of his company. And the business address I already knew.

But in the very end it was simple after all. In a large brown Dumpster I was looking for objects that might assist me, in particular waterproof clothing or a tent. Tents were nowhere, and I needed a new one more than anything.

While I was hunting, turning things over with my rubber-gloved hands, I came across a pile of old telephone books, among some plaid cushions that were trailing pieces of foam stuffing. I barely noticed them at first and continued in my search, finding nothing except a brand-new toothbrush still in its package. This I pocketed gratefully.

But then I stopped and turned and picked up a phonebook. It was from twelve years before Mr. D. had first found me.

I looked up his name, and there it was listed, with an address.

I had a worn map of the city and enough coins for the bus. It was a few hours before the first light of dawn but I went to the address right away. From the bus stop I walked until I got to the right number on the right street.

It was a large and upright house on a lawn with high hedges. In front of it there was a FOR SALE sign.

I crept alongside this straight, tall house between it and the next, along a driveway that was overgrown by weeds. And I looked into a window, because I had to, and then another. But there were curtains and blinds on each one.

So I had to wait until it got light to knock on the door. Or I might be taken for a shameless felon again.

I lay beside a hedge and waited several hours, until some cars began crawling and purring along the streets. And then I saw a man come out of the front door, bald with almost no chin and holding a briefcase. He passed close by me, and I could smell shaving cream and see that his socks had blue diamonds on them.

And he got into a car that was parked on the street and started the engine.

After he pulled away I got up and brushed the grass off my stomach and elbows and small twigs out of my hair. And I knocked on the door.

When the woman in the quilted housecoat opened it, she said, "Forget your keys?" before she looked at me. Then she squeaked.

"Excuse me," I said.

"Who the hell are you?" she asked.

But she calmed down when I said I was an old friend of Mr. D. Then she looked at me from my head to my feet, and I could tell she felt the overalls were not all they should be.

"Fallen on hard times," I added. I did not believe my times were harder than the next. However I have often found that people like to hear apologies.

"Oh," she said. And nodded her head. "In that case I have sad news for you. He recently passed away. His heart gave out."

It took me by surprise. I had not considered this. Everyone was dying. And I said Brother's name without thinking: it lurched out.

But she did not appear to notice my disarray, only stepped past me and picked up the rolled newspaper in a blur of light blue. I had gone porous, crumbling. Her slippers had exploding puffs on the toes.

"His son? He has a new legal guardian. It's a lawyer somewhere. He goes to boarding school and then camp in the summer. In England or something, I don't know, far away."

Relief was the falling of gravity. So my knees buckled beneath me.

Later she was leaning over, worried because I had hit my skull on the walkway. There was an ache, but it was nothing. She was concerned but also embarrassed I could tell, looking this way and that to see if the neighbors had noticed me.

She had brought a wet rag out of the house while I was lying there and now plied it on my forehead. I felt the trickle into my hair, where the drops grew cool as stones on the skin. And I was calmer than I had been in years.

She said, as she was helping me to get up with a hand under my arm, that she was the housekeeper who used to keep the house for Mr. D. and rented it out for him too, once he grew too wealthy to live there himself. And now that he was dead, she was still keeping the house until it was sold and living in it for free.

"Do you have any pictures of him?" I asked.

She thought I meant Mr. D. Anyway, she had no pictures of Brother and had never met him personally.

"But," she said confidentially, "I hear he was adopted. Why, did you meet the kid?"

And finally I shook my head.

But I was happy to know of him.

I knew Brother still existed. And that was enough for me.

I left soon because there was no more conversation between us, only hanging questions of what to say. I thanked her and walked away with the buzz of relief in my veins, warming me. It circulated for a long time, as I considered Brother going about his life. Unhurt and possibly happy.

And I was able to leave Brother finally, knowing he was safe. I left him wherever he was and could be.

Blue Oval

I was used to having a destination. So without one I was unsure what to do, and I was in no rush. I had noticed I was becoming invisible, or rather translucent. And I was interested in watching this. I had just begun to observe that, as I grew older, I was fading in the eyes of men. A face seemed to me to act as plumage. It is brilliant when people are young and then begins to fade: so people grow less visible as they age, at least to younger ones. With wrinkles in the skin the planes cease to reflect the light readily, and the brightness of the face is dimmed.

I was grateful to be spoken to, and very pleased to listen, on those occasions when I was so fortunate as not to be alone. But fewer and fewer people would talk to me. It was almost as though there were rules against it. I had encountered many rules about affection in the past but never understood them. Apparently it is finite and thus not to be shared recklessly. And that is the law.

But myself I had never known this. Feeling seemed to me without bounds and vast, formless and not taking up space. I never liked thinking of wasted hands that reach and find no object. Trembling and suspended.

And yet fewer and fewer people tended to speak to me.

Anyway, I was considering this carefully during the days. And I slept on the bench at night until some kind and wise policemen offered to take me with them.

"It's not a tropical vacation," said one policeman, "but it's better than this."

I told them I preferred the bench, thinking they suspected me of a new felony. But they said only how cold it was, which was true, and how the cold was not welcoming. So they took me to a place where I was given soup and bread to eat, and then a bed to sleep on, alongside many others. And there were other people there, but when I spoke to them they seemed to be quite absent, after all.

The next morning I was told of another place I should take myself to, so I did. And there they asked me many questions as I sat beneath the long white tubes of light, but without trying to make me say I had committed a felony. A kind woman wearing a plastic name card asked me if I had an occupation currently. I told her that I did not. However once in my youth, I said, I had been quite accustomed to cleaning and tidying.

And then she smiled and said she knew a place where I could go: and it was a hotel.

At first I was uncertain about this suggestion, since I no longer had any money left to pay for hotels. But when I got there with my box I saw that this was not a hotel such as I knew, for it was only full of men, alone, who lived there for a time without paying.

And there a second woman showed me to a room that opened from a door beneath a stairway. It was a small room, but it seemed excellent to me. It had a slim bed and one window, high up on the wall beyond my reach. And then she showed me to the closet where they kept the mops, and brooms, and the coarse powders and blue solutions.

I was pleased because the smell of coarse powder and the wet gray strands of mops recalled me to my friends of long ago.

*And so I was established there and cleaned again, dur-*ing the days. The building of the men's hostel was warm with all the exhalations of people, their breathing and relief from cold in the winter; and this warmth tended also to fill me. The men would amble through the halls nodding. Some would pat my shoulder and inquire as to my welfare. Because they were alone and without company, I was very fond of these tired men who came and went. After a time I even had some wrinkled dollar bills that I was paid, and with them I bought myself a black box that played music. It stood on a wooden table that I had pulled out of a pile of broken wood on the curb and placed beside my bed.

I found that it was pleasant to go through the rooms, one at a time, and scour them till their floors shone and the glass of their windows was clear. Because each room was an occasion, full and whole. It bore the smudges and the soft marks of habitation of the tired men. The lived-in rooms with smudges and disorder were the round end of a life, and clean ones were an opening.

Sadly, the tired men did not often stay long but soon had to be going. Then after some weeks or months they would be back again, even more tired than they had been before they left. And they would shake their heads rue-fully at me.

One of these men could not see too well. He wore old glasses all the time, with very thick yellow glass, and was thin as a stick. He left and then came back again, until I knew what he would want when he returned, and how he liked his room to be. In the room I placed a broken wind chime that I found, with one disk missing from its oval chimes, which were of blackened silver metal with blue glass inside. He liked this wind chime, so that when he came back and his room was already full, and he was assigned to a different room, I moved the wind chime with him. I would run to the new room before he got there and hang the chime from a hook, stealthily.

I believe he thought all of the rooms had wind chimes, each the same as the next, with one blue circle missing in their metal eyes whose absence he could hear.

And by and by this man James asked me if I would read to him. He brought a small dog-eared bundle out of his olive green knapsack. It was letters, held together with elastic bands, that were very old and worn and written on lined paper, brown on the edges. And he asked me to read them aloud, one by one. He said that in past days, when his eyesight was strong, he had read the letters himself. But now he wished to remember what they said.

So for a while every night I went to his room that he shared, and the others who also slept in the room would curl up quiet behind me on their beds. And I would read an old letter to him by the bedside lamp. I sat on a straight-backed chair next to his cot and he lay on his back and closed his eyes.

The letters were all from the same person, who after a time I learned had been his wife. They did not describe grand events, but rather only a day or an hour or the weather and what was thought on that day, in its moments. Or sometimes there would be a word or a phrase that someone else had said, to the wife of James or in her hearing as she wrote the letter, such as *The rain will come and soak the sheets*. And while I read most times, James often fell asleep.

He told me one night that his wife was dead, and had been dead so long that she was growing faint. And sometimes he almost forgot she had been. And when he realized he was forgetting, he would be struck by the fear that she had never existed. And that she was now lost and alone in the limbo of unremembered people. And that this was his fault.

Also, he said, when she was alive he was away from her more often than not. He drove a truck across the country. It was a poultry truck and often full of chickens in cages. And as he drove across the country he would pick up the letters in different cities, which she sent to him at General Delivery. He was gone forty-two weeks of the year.

He did not even like chickens, he told me.

So when she died he went hollow, he said. He was haunted because he had not watched her living. And he insisted to me that if a life was not seen it disappeared utterly. And why people got married, he said, was to have an observer.

And I thought, So as not to be invisible.

Anyway, he liked to hear the old letters, since he could not read them anymore. By means of the letters he could watch her life that was already gone, which at the time he had missed. And by him observing it, the life would be real and she would not have never existed.

But one night as I was reading I forgot the room and wind chimes. And the buckets and the mops and the blue solutions. As I read I was sliding, and felt no solid things. For I had left my bones, and left my skin.

I looked up and around the room at the other men lying curled on their beds, some with their knees drawn up to their chests. And for a second I thought I was seeing the future, when they shed their bodies. And then I thought: No it is not the future. Rather it is the pasts they regret, and it is these men revealed. In place of each I saw the insubstantial man, who was his own dream of himself.

Each of them had a shape that turned and moved around him twisting and floating, with arms that were not arms and tongues that were not tongues. They were the others that they wished they could have been, and I was among them too and we all intersected. The threads of all our forms touched close between us, whether or not we knew.

So gradually, when I went each night to read the letters out loud, I became the wife of sad James. And neither did

I cease to be myself, for that was impossible. But at the same moment I was both her and me as I read, and the walls of both our selves had softened. And this conviction stayed with me even when I had finished reading.

Once James held his hands out to me, and I took them. Then I lay on the bed with him. So we were closer than skin.

And when James was snoring and holding his pillow to his front as he slept, I left the room quietly in my sock feet.

And when I lay in my own small room planning to go to sleep, with its one window high above my head, I was not alone anymore, as I am not alone here. The walls had become transparent.

And I could see through them even without windows.

So I saw that this was what it meant to be invisible, that the other people no longer saw you but it did not matter. Because now you saw all of them perfectly, what they were as well as what they had been and would be.

And so in this way I discovered that I had reached my destination already. And I did not need to depart.

By and by James left the hostel again and was gone, with all his letters that he kept in his knapsack. Soon after that the kindly woman who had given me my room the first day, and showed me where the closet was in which the blue solutions stayed, told me the hostel would be closed.

Because, she said, the kindness of the state had other work to do. And now the men should feed themselves. And then, she said, there would no longer be a need to clean the hostel, for no men would come there, and so I too would be asked to leave.

I told her that I would be quite content to stay, in any case, and clean for the new people. But then she shook her head and said that this would not be possible, unfortunately. She said the building would change hands, and others from the government would have their offices there and turn its rooms and halls to other purposes.

And they had their own cleaning ladies.

"I do have a question I need to ask you," she said as I was rising to leave the interview. "Uh, one of the men told me that you mentioned something about hallucinations?"

"Not that I know of," I said.

"You said you saw forms behind some of the men?"

So I tipped my head to one side and said oh yes. And she asked me if the forms had claws or horns or were hairy.

I said, "Excuse me, hairy?"

She went on to ask if they were frightening demons and if they said anything to me, such as telling me what to do.

When I stared at her, she asked, "Have they given you orders?"

I laughed and said I certainly hoped not.

I said, "It was a figure of speech."

And she nodded and said, "Uh-huh. I see."

· · ·

Then the day came when all the tired men had left, and no one was there, and I too had to leave. I gathered up my cardboard box and music box, my towel and my tooth, and I also took the wind chimes, since they were not needed anymore by the kindness of the state.

I was preparing to go back to the bench, for it was summer and there was no risk of freezing.

But all at once, nervously, the same kindly woman now told me I would not go to the bench, but should wait, and other people would come to get me and take me to a hospital, which was also run by the government. She asked if that was all right.

I asked, just to make sure, if she thought they would let me clean up there, in exchange for room and board.

She said, "Uh, they just might."

I said, "Thank you so much for everything."

And she left.

So I waited sitting on the front steps, hoping that the hospital people would also give me a warm and quiet room with thick, throbbing walls, and show me where a closet was full of cleaning items so that I could lend assistance. This had been such a good home for me.

By and by the hospital people came, driving a van. And I got in and went with them. They drove until we were quite far away, and there were fences and enormous lakes of parking lots; there was also a vast gray building like so many boxes stacked one above the other. And when I asked if I would be cleaning the halls and the rooms there, they said not exactly.

However, they said, I would live there and get help.

And as it happens I still live there to this day.

And now and then I recall the letters from James's wife, whom I never knew but sometimes was. And for no reason I am prone to recite to myself, as though I were still reading: *The rain will come and soak the sheets.*

So on occasion before I fall asleep I think of sheets, so wet that water pours off them forever. I think the sheets were hanging from a line and rain came with dark clouds and soaked them; but then I think that when the clouds retired, and the sun returned, water poured down from the hems of the sheets even beneath the great bright sun. And through the days and months and years that followed in the sun, which someday will be centuries, the water still pours off those sheets. It comes from nowhere steadily.

4

It did not strike me as soon as it should have that my bed was not set in stone. Because the four heavy black metal legs and the long sides of the frame, which contained the springs that the mattress rested on, were bolted together tightly.

But I was lying on the floor staring up at the ceiling one morning recently—morning for me that is—and happened to move my head idly so that it lay beneath the springs. I noticed cobwebs on their tight wire coils, though I have never seen a spider in this room. Certainly I would have welcomed one. And then I noticed that the bolts that attached the tops of the legs to the bottom of the frame were brown with rust and flaking. So I reached out and grasped one of them and twisted it.

At first it did not budge. But on the second try it moved slightly. And very small flakes of rust, brittle as black paint, came off on my crushed fingertips.

I am already weak with slow movements and slack muscles. But the lateness of the find is not a surprise to me. Often I have learned the name of some small, lovely animal just as it went extinct.

I slid out from under the bed, raised myself up on my bruised knees, and pulled the mattress off the springs and onto the floor. Then I hefted the bed frame up onto its side. And I kneeled and went to work unscrewing the first bolt painstakingly, and then the second. And soon I had a leg. It was a heavy bar whose base was still sharp at the corners.

I chose the wall that contained the door because I suspected it was the thinnest. I did not know what the other three walls gave onto, but this one gave onto the hallway outside. And I recalled all the leaving noises that I had heard through it and guessed it might not be too thick.

The first swing made a scar in the plaster that was shaped like an *L*, peaked in a roof with point upward. I flushed and saw black suns and had to sit down on the floor quickly. The contact stunned me and I was vibrating.

I went and drank from the sink, long and deep. I was so thirsty and hurried that I hit my front teeth on the tap.

And then I went back to the wall and swung again.

I have been doing it for a day or two now, I think. As a rest from the effort I sleep or I write, though I am down to three short pencils and one nub of eraser. I frequently erase what I have written as soon as it embarrasses me. And when I am ready for heavy lifting again I pick up the black bar and bang it into the crater I have made, trying to force an opening.

I could have punished myself for not having thought of this sooner. For clearly if I had begun to hit the wall when I still had food in my body, and was not steadily dwindling and shrinking, I would have opened a hole in no time. But then, unlike a soldier, I was never trained to see weapons in everyday objects.

And as you may have noticed from my life, although happy, it was also rife with stupidity, so this is fitting. Early man learned to use tools, it said in the encyclopedia. And this made him different from the beasts. But often he does not choose to use them. Especially when he is stupid.

Sometimes I remember the ocean. And I know it does not remember me. And I think about how it has never known a loss, but only was and continues to be. As far as I have been informed. Still, I do not envy the ocean. I wonder if eternity is worth it.

Of course I am wistful at the drop of a hat and always imagining. Now from time to time, as I chop away at the stubborn plaster with stringy, pale arms flinging the bed leg in abandon, I think that when I finally break through, the hallway I remember with its linoleum and its windows that are sealed shut will be gone. And in its place an ocean that turns out, after all these years, to remember. When I step out through the broken wall the world will be full of movement. Nothing will not have feeling; even the dirt will laugh.

Or so I make up.

Also, since I broke down the bed, I have become curious about the pipes.

I would never take apart the sink; I need the water that courses up through its black swan neck. Water is my single help. But I can do without showers if I have to, I decided, on the chance that I might find, in the pipes or faucets, a sharp and useful thing. I was hoping for a hook-shaped part, which I would try to attach to the end of my bar with a twisted bedspring. My razor blade was already dull from sharpening pencils.

So I have managed to remove the upper pair of faucets in the bathtub by unscrewing them. I have pulled up the white tiles around these faucets by digging at the soft lines between them. And I can see the pipes receding, small tunnels into the wall and far away. I even put my mouth around one of them and called down into the dark. But there was no echo.

I have thought of flooding the bathroom in the hope that the water would soak the floor and collapse it, and I could leave here that way. However, in the event that the floor of the building is too strong and fortified to sag under the weight of the water, I do not wish to spend the rest of my days ankle deep and blue with the cold, teeth chattering.

So I have decided to settle for the tool I already have, and continue to hit the wall. The palms of my hands are sore with red ridges, but there is something to show for it: a shallow crater and beneath it a dusting of white powder on the gray linoleum.

Bracelet

After the nurses put the bracelet with its snap on my wrist, I had to fill out a long sheet of paper on a clipboard. I did not know any of the answers, which were numbers, it seemed, all pertaining to me. I did have a passport; the old man had bought it for me long ago and left it in the hotel with the stacks of money. It had a helpful number stamped on it out of small holes and a birth date, which I believe he must have invented since it made me appear several years older than I was supposed to be.

An orderly was charged with taking me to my room, but he was not talkative. Instead he was listening to a game of something on his headphones. Now and then I would hear a faint wave of cheering.

As we stood beside each other in the elevator I asked him, "Excuse me. How many cleaning women do they have here?"

But he only adjusted the volume.

Since the elevator did not stop soon but kept rising through several floors, and I saw a map on the wall that showed how enormous the hospital was, I decided there must be many cleaning persons: an army of them.

We walked along several halls with the orderly saying, "Hey, Ron," to another orderly in passing and "Whatup," to a nurse but still nothing to me. Then we turned and went in a door. And I saw a long row of beds. The orderly tapped one of them with his pen and nodded. And on the end of the bed was yet another clipboard, this one empty.

I soon discovered there was another room that we could go to. It was devoted to recreation, and the nurse called it the rec room. It contained a potted plant with white stripes on the leaves, games such as checkers and Parcheesi, crayons and colored paper, six large books with pictures in them, and a xylophone.

Shoes

After a while there were too many walls and not enough doors. And every day I woke up and looked into a tunnel. The same paths were walked, with bright red and green and yellow lines on the floors and the ceilings to tell me where to put my feet. I wore white paper shoes with ruffles around the elastic on my ankles. In these shoes there was nothing to do but shuffle. All moving was shuffling.

Also the sun was almost never in view, neither the sun nor the moon was visible but only the long bright tubes and the squares and angles and corners of the building.

I did not wish to be ungrateful, but certain procedures were performed on me repeatedly.

So then what happened was that things dispersed, and I forgot what was real since nothing appeared to be. And the forms that had been ideas in the first place turned into absent friends. I saw them at surprising times, gesturing to me. The forms were wide and light and without name, which made them confusing. Sometimes I would see names in them, but the names would make no sense. They were the names of places I never had seen and persons who had never noticed me. I would walk around beneath the yellow lines or the blue ones reaching out for forms that disappeared, always hoping that they would touch me.

In the recreation room there was a television, and always on the screen were warm colors and rooms full of persons who were never alone in their lives but always surrounded by others. These others touched them and stayed with them at all times, being their families. And there was laughing commonly. I had noticed this before, that there were warm-colored lives in boxes, full of company, but I had thought it was not possible for me. Now I was missing what I had not missed before.

It was because of all the walls I believe, and having no land or wind around me.

So I began to enter the rooms of others at the hospital. I would walk into them at night looking for friends who were not absent for once, or I would stare during the visiting hours at those who came and went and those who never had visitors at all. I would notice the ones who were left, and later, if they were still alone, I would go and stay for a long time with them, talking and sitting. And if one put her arms around me I would tuck myself into them. Several were prone to do this and we would lie side by side.

There was Gottfried, who did not like to walk but preferred to pull himself across the floor using his hands and elbows, with his thin legs, long and slack, dragging behind. Plus there was his friend Randall K., who was often inclined to roll into a ball. And there was a small plump man who would often say he was famous and thank you, his name was Fidel Castro. But other times he was modest and was only Fidel Castro's secretary. And that was easier because then he did not have to go around puffing on a plastic spoon as though it was a fine cigar. And when he was Fidel Castro's secretary he stood upright and acted prim. When he was the secretary he held his hands up in front of his chest like the paws of a rabbit.

Sometimes I would be found by some nurse or orderly and taken back to my room while I was sitting speaking to the ones who were likewise without company, such as Gottfried or Fidel Castro. There was a doctor who did not take to my wandering and spoke to me harshly, saying let them be. And he wished we would all stay in our rooms separately. His name was Dr. Sen.

Dr. Sen was always very busy. He was tired from being busy and sometimes would speak quite sharply. He was even so exhausted that he would forget things, such as who was who, or what he believed was terribly wrong with them.

Still often I could stay with other people, when Dr. Sen was too busy to notice me. And then I would not see the forms floating and hovering, but rather I would see the person I was with and speak only to him, and the quiet would recede all around and we would be together.

It was one night when I had stayed with Gottfried until very late, and was shuffling back in my slippers along the dim hall with the red EXIT lights shining across the floor now and then, that I first saw Brother again.

He was still very small. I saw he was walking so he was not an infant anymore, but he was only a child. He was two or three maybe, though I do not know too much about the ages of children. He was at the end of the hall under a window, and behind him outside were the trees.

And the first thing I thought when I saw him was: My life has been an illusion. And look, no time has passed in all these years.

I said, "Brother!"

And I picked up my shuffling feet till I felt there was no floor. And my robe was flying, I thought, behind me.

But he turned and rose as I came nearer to him and left by the window, flowing straight through the glass and up into the trees as though he was a part of them.

Where he had been there was only dust on the floor.

After that I would often see Brother.

I saw him walking out of dark corners with his head down, and running toward me from the burning centers of lights with his soft eyes wide open. He would also come out of strangers, out of their arms or shoulders or stepping away from their legs like a shadow separating from a body. He would descend from a painting on a wall or pull together from the folds of curtains and be coming toward me. But he always dissolved before I got to him.

I grew upset with all this dissolving. And though before I had done without him, now I was seeing him everywhere but not touching him. And it was worse than having nothing.

And I thought his open eyes were questions and his palms were open as though he needed help. Sometimes I was worried that something had happened to him; at other times I thought the Brother I was seeing was an old Brother who had been shucked like a skin while the new one kept going through time. So that he was a discarded Brother, an unwanted figment left behind by the seasons.

He began to pass me all the time, too far away and yet so close that I could feel his breath. I chased him, falling when he faded too fast. I would find myself on the ground often. And Dr. Sen was always gruff and liked to pull me by the wrist.

If there was a whole day when Brother was not seen, I would go looking for him among all the forms that lined the halls and shrank and flocked away from me at night.

Once, at the end of such a day, a large crowd gathered in the parking lot. The sun was going down and so all the cars had golden windows. Through the window in the recreation room, where I had been reading a certain large book I had read many times before, I saw them down there in the parking lot, all gazing up at some point above me. I saw their faces with squinting eyes and their white coats.

And usually we were not permitted into the parking lot and certainly not so late. But this occasion would be different, I saw, since the doctors, nurses, and orderlies were all down there and were not watching me.

So I closed the book and shuffled to the elevator. I pressed the button marked G and went down in my paper shoes and my robe to join them. Then I shuffled through the lobby, and everyone was so occupied with tasks at the desks that they did nothing to slow my progress.

And I went around the corner of the building, tearing the bottoms of my paper shoes on the cement. The crowd was gathered looking up at the roof. Besides the doctors and nurses there were other patients. The nurses and the orderlies were very anxious, and Dr. Sen was talking through a bullhorn. But through the buzzing and the resounding it was impossible to hear his words.

I looked up at where they were gazing. And high on the roof near the edge was a small dark figure.

And I knew at once it was Brother.

There was someone behind him, a white shape beck-oning. And on one side of the crowd were firemen unrolling something. But I did not look at the white shape, and I barely saw the firemen either. I only kept my eyes on Brother, and I walked up through the crowd to the front row, nearest the wall of the building. One nurse whis-pered, "Get back. Stay back." But I did not pay too much attention because my eyes were fixed on the small dark figure.

So I saw how Brother stepped up to the rim of the roof. And the people in the crowd all surged forward murmuring.

I thought I would finally get to touch him, and that he was ready to be with me.

So I called, "Excuse me. Brother! Please come here!"

And I reached out too.

Then Brother looked at me, spread his arms wide, and turned his face up. And he fell.

A few nights after that, an old and bent orderly led me out of the room with the long row of beds to a far smaller room, tucked at the end of a dim corridor. I could not even say good-bye because the orderly moved me so early in the morning that all the others I knew were still occu-pied sleeping.

He brought my shoebox of possessions, and presently he also brought my old thin towel with its holes.

Knees

After they put me in the small room they kept locked all the time, I tried to find things to do while I waited. I kept expecting Dr. Sen to come visit me and tell me what he called a prognosis. However, instead of coming to visit me himself, he only sent a message or an item now and then through the very ancient orderly whose name was Ali.

And Ali said that Dr. Sen was very angry at me. And he said the patient on the roof was the doctor's own personal friend.

And I said, "Please forgive me. It was a mistake. I thought he was someone who was taken from me."

Ali bent his head and said he knew that it was not my fault. But still Dr. Sen was angry.

I said, "I am better now. I promise."

But Ali would not look at me.

Once the doctor sent me a clear globe of silver rain falling on a city. And at the bottom was written CHICAGO. Another time he sent a blue rubber ball, which bounced and rolled until it lodged against the wall and then was still.

And after that he sent me something strange, that is, a bone from a chicken. It was cooked and still wet and Ali placed it in the middle of the floor and then retired, closing the door behind him. It was a wishbone, I believe. I only sat looking at it, believing it was none of my business.

Presently I asked Ali what this meant, and he shrugged his shoulders and seemed to be embarrassed. Because we did not know what the code should signify.

And always the next day Dr. Sen made Ali take these items away. For the sake of my perfect aloneness, he said. And once he told Ali, who did not speak English perfectly, to inform me that this was isolation therapy and was I enjoying it. Or maybe that was not what Ali said, as I could not always discern his words.

But on his own Ali let me have several items that he brought in to me, including a small brown alarm clock that ran on two batteries. And by following the hours on the clock, I could record the passing of days and even count them. Because although I had never before had a fondness for numbers, there were few distractions now and I counted slowly. So I knew that it had been just over four months and a week when Ali disappeared without a warning.

I wondered if it was his heart since he had a murmur, he had told me. I was worried for Ali. I mused over his disappearing, though I was not surprised because all people were prone to go away from me finally.

I thought he had said to me the last morning, "He will let you out of here." However, later I was remembering Ali's wrinkled face with purple bags under his tired eyes. And I almost thought, for a second, it might have been, "We will get you out of here."

But this would never be clear.

• • •

And then another orderly named Jim, who was younger and not from another country, started bringing in my food trays to me. And soon after I met Jim the batteries in the clock were used up. So time stopped.

Jim never brought me any messages from Dr. Sen. He said Dr. Sen had ceased addressing himself to me. However there were still his instructions. And he said that I could not have books, games, pictures of the world, or paper to write on. In fact I was not permitted to see anything more of the outside. Not at all.

Jim said he would make an exception for me if I promised to hide what I had under my bed if anyone should come to the door. Although no one ever did.

And so he brought me a gardening magazine one week, and the next week he took it away and brought me a thin section from a local newspaper, which had a listing of *Deaths Deaths Deaths* across the top. It was obituaries. I remembered all of them for a while, up to the last in the column, which was cut off by the torn edge of the paper. *Shapiro— Rose G. Beloved wife of the late Benjamin, dear mother of Dorothy and Tim, she reached out her hand and brought light into our darkest moments. In lieu of flowers please send*

I would lie on my side on the floor some nights until I could feel it grown warm beneath me and feel the hum of the furnace that heated the building, throbbing through the floor. Beside me I would hold the cardboard box I had come in. And I would hold the blue oval between my thumb and forefinger and wonder if I was becoming less insane yet and when I could go free. I would let myself float, adrift in the soft memories.

And I would say to Jim in the morning, "When is the isolation therapy going to end?" Or I would ask him how I could show Dr. Sen that I knew who was my brother and who was not my brother at all. Because after the fall Dr. Sen had shaken his head and said again and again to me, "He was not your brother. Not your brother at all."

And Jim would get shifty with his glances and kick at the doorjamb and say he only worked here. Then he would ask me if I wanted a stupid magazine or not. And he would say, "All I got today's one on home electronics."

Finally Jim went away also, on a vacation. He told me he was going to the Bahamas. And he was planning on swimming underwater with a tube to breathe through. And he would see the striped fishes and the coral reefs in the blue water and the waving green weeds. Also he would drink several drinks that were very brightly colored and featured very small umbrellas.

The doctor would arrange for another orderly, he said. But he did not know who it would be. And he would be gone for three weeks, but then he would return.

So while I was sleeping one night, there was a click and then I woke up and the door closed, but still there were not any lights. I said, "Jim? Are you back?"

But there was only the sound of feet scraping, and breathing in the dark. I sat up in my bed and pushed the sheets away from my legs. Then there was a hoarse whisper and the warmth of near bodies and a light in my face. I turned away blinking and then turned back, and I saw it was a flashlight. Holding the flashlight was a woman with long hair, and behind her was Dr. Sen. He looked different because he was not wearing the white coat he always wore but rather a black coat with a different shape, and he was carrying a bottle that I recognized contained a fine intoxicant.

And in the woman's brown hair there were gray streaks. She was wearing a long dress and shoes with heels so tall and thin that she swayed and wobbled as she leaned over me.

They both had an unfamiliar smell, of onions and smoke and something crumbling beneath the ground.

"There she is," said Dr. Sen to the woman. "That's her."

And the woman stepped up to me and shone the light in my face so I had to close my eyes.

"So this is her," said the woman slowly, and put down her flashlight on the bed beside me and fumbled with the glittery bag that hung from her shoulder. She pulled out a pack of cigarettes and lit one. Then she inhaled from it and leaned close to me and said, "You're the one."

I was quiet because I did not know what she meant. And she stared at me and smoked again, and the orange end glowed.

"She doesn't look that bad," said the woman, flicking her ash.

And Dr. Sen said, "None of them do."

So they stared at me closely, with the woman blowing thin plumes of smoke through her nostrils.

And finally I asked, "Is it time for me to go now?"

Then Dr. Sen giggled and stopped suddenly and took a gulp from his bottle. He said, "Yes. Time for you to go now. So get up."

And he snapped the sheets off my feet, so they billowed up quickly and fell on the floor. And I stepped out of bed.

Then each of them took one of my arms, as though they did not wish me to walk alone. And Dr. Sen carried the bottle with him, and the woman leaned down and took the flashlight and put it in her bag and smoked her cigarette as she walked beside me.

I was so pleased to leave my room for once that at first I did not notice how fast we were going, that they were pulling me forward with their fingernails digging into the skin of my wrists. But I noticed the woman started hiccuping and crying as she smoked, and then she would laugh. And I wondered what she was thinking.

So we went quickly up some stairs, four and five and six flights until we were in front of a heavy metal door with a flat red bar across it that said DO NOT OPEN EXCEPT

IN CASE OF EMERGENCY. And Dr. Sen put a key in the lock on the door and turned it.

My feet were bare, so when we stepped out onto the roof they were cold on the soles.

But I saw the stars and was giddy. We all stopped and looked up at them. And the woman flung her cigarette down onto the roof and stamped on it, but her sharp heel went through the roofing and she stumbled and shrieked and said, "Shit shit shit!" But then she laughed and cried again. And when she was steady she reached across me, took the bottle from Dr. Sen, and drank from it.

After that she was quiet and leaned backward and looked up at Orion. And she said, "I miss him."

So then Dr. Sen pulled me across the roof. And we went up to the edge, and I could see over it, down into the parking lot where the crowd had been standing. But now it was empty, with only two tall lights that cast broad white circles on the concrete around them, and a few cars parked in the far corners.

And Dr. Sen said, "Do you know where we are?"

I said, "On the roof."

And Dr. Sen said, "This is where he jumped from. When you waved to him."

I said, "But I know it wasn't Brother. And I am still so sorry."

The woman said, "Oh you're sorry."

And she came up behind me and took hold of my other arm again. Then both of them pressed me forward so that I was dangling. My feet were still on the edge of the roof, but my body was dangling over. My arms became sore right away and felt as though they might be prone to tear off.

I felt my heart beating fast, and I wanted to look up to see the constellations, such as the winged horse and the swan, which I always have loved. But it was difficult to raise my head so far above the horizon. And Dr. Sen was talking, and the woman was crying and coughing, but I could not hear what she said with the rushing in my ears and my heart racing from the distance that I was above the ground, and the weight of the hanging.

So I only muttered to myself, "If I could just see a bit more."

And Dr. Sen began to shout, "You see? You see?"

But I could not see anything except the parking lot.

And my wrists were aching as well as my shoulders.

Then all at once my legs were rubber underneath me, and one of my feet slipped off the edge. And I pitched forward. The woman screamed, and Dr. Sen grabbed me suddenly around my waist and pulled back on me. And we all collapsed on the edge of the roof. The woman was on top of me on the grainy surface, so that my knees scraped beneath me. My chin hit the edge where I had been dangling, and I bit my tongue.

And then the woman was on my back still screaming, and pulled my arms behind me and breathed hard on the back of my neck, sobbing and whispering. And her breathing was all over me, in my ears and on my skin with onions and strangeness. And then she started to pummel me with her fists, like Caesar used to.

And I felt myself swallowing all the warm blood from my tongue, which stung where I had bitten through it. And I waited through the pummeling until I think I fell asleep.

Later I woke up in the bathtub in my room with warm water running over my ankles. My feet had been raised up and propped against the porcelain. I could see black blood caked along the nails and between the toes, spread so the dried drips fanned out like river deltas. I guessed it was where they had been dragged on the roof. My knees were ragged and still covered in bright red over the flesh, burning and stinging. And there was a bar of green soap floating beside me in the shallow water. I recalled the faint sound of a door closing again and a key turning just as I was waking up.

When my tongue stopped bleeding, I could breathe more easily, although there was no moving cool air as there had been on the roof but only the thick stillness of walls around me. But I could still not move my arms or my legs. They were stiff with soreness, and I could bend my neck just enough to see rings of dark black bruises on my legs.

So I lay there for a long, long time after the water had grown cold. I could not move and I was quite hungry. And every now and then I would slowly lift my cupped hands and drink the water from the bath.

There were itches that spidered across my body, and my voice rose out of my mouth and echoed across the tiles in waves. Then in the lulls there was silence. And me clearing my throat in short coughs. I had conversations with absent friends, and there was enough time for almost every song I had heard in my life. But of each of them I only knew two or three lines. Such as a song that Mrs. Ray had taught me, by a famous Protestant she said. "A mighty fortress is our God, a bulwark never fay-ay-ay-ling."

But finally I was tired of the songs.

And all I thought about as I lay there shivering was people who had never been born. I thought that in never being born, these kind and wise people had always been asleep. They had spent their whole lives waiting for the beginning. And I thought: There is one birth of bones and skin, and then there is another, I believe. And the second birth is the birth of the dream.

Anyway, when I could move my arms I finally ran new water and made myself warm again. And after a time I could even get up and haul myself out of the bathroom and wrap myself in the sheets again, which I picked up off the floor. And I came to feel a fondness for my plum-colored rough knees, the same fondness I feel for my twisted foot. I think they are so ugly they are beautiful again.

And by the time that Jim returned there were dark scabs on my knees and my bruises had faded and turned yellow.

Jim's face was solid brown like plastic. He had many pictures of himself drinking colorful drinks that featured umbrellas and cherries and parrots made out of pipe cleaners. Smiling he told me about the coral reefs he had seen and the heavy sea turtles swimming with slow oars of legs. And he told me about the harmless sharks with long teeth.

Air

Sometimes I think there must be a vast number of rooms like this one, with doors that are not prone to open. And then I breathe in, and the past comes back to me. But I cannot see which past it is. I only draw a breath and have the feeling I have been here before, wherever I am. It is too much for me. At such times I almost believe that everywhere is one place, and that is the place of memory, and I walk through and I catch glimpses of myself. And others mill around also, wandering and remembering. It may be a garden or the bank of a river, where I have been and not been, both at once. Or I believe it is another person's past I am recalling then, another person's memory has drifted to me on the breeze as though it were my own.

But I have also found that memories fly away in broad-winged flocks. They fly toward the west and lose shape in the sun. And though the memory has lost the feathers of its wings, and so cannot be seen exactly as it was, those wings still churn the air.

And this evening—or so I believe it is, though I do not have proof—I learned something that I had never known before. The room was dark because one of my lightbulbs has finally winked out and I am saving the other for writing and hammering. And I was lying on the floor resting for a time, with my shoulders aching and my palms burning hard from gripping the metal bar, and I gazed at the dark walls.

And as I looked the walls turned into sky. There were no stars and no constellations, but I knew anyway that the walls had turned transparent for good this time and would never be solid again.

So I was not alone. With me were the absent people. And all of them were not bodies but only the forms of all their sorrow and longing. By and by I felt what I had always known, that myself I was neither a city nor a rock, but only particles and figments. And like all people I was quite imaginary when I was alone. And alone we were all of us ghosts.

But I could simply disappear and nothing would have changed. And when I saw this, I laughed in the dark and felt happier than ever. I thought of how people wish to be singular, so as to feel that, being gone, they still will not be gone. And I thought this was fine and as it should be. And I wished all the wistful people good fortune, and said out loud that I at least would still remember them, and do my best through all the years. I said to myself, I will hold them dear and dear and dear, until, at last, I forget everything.

So then among the walls that were not walls I got up from where I had been lying down, though this was difficult, since I have shrunk. I crashed the bar into the center of the crater in the wall. I almost think I am on to something. I almost think I can detect the end of it, the thin end. I can almost step out.

A soft memory can be a far memory or it can be a near one, though mostly a soft memory is far, and not solid. Its lines are not distinct, its colors are dark, its taste is salty and sweet. A soft memory may also be a dream, as I have said. I do not always know which is which. For instance now, since I have been alone so long, I remember affection.

And then I think I may only have dreamed.

But I have seen all the forms of dreams before me. And that is quite enough. I always have been fortunate, and now I am still happier than I have been before. Because while I am insisting, even now banging away in the dark stupidly, I can see all the lovely forms. And anyway, as I do what I have to, a vanished person comes to me and whispers: You do not have to wish to be forever. Because we all are here, he says, and it is warm.

And look at that. Look at them all, passing and moving in their quick moments of not being gone, and the wind blowing on the wild fields. But you and I have always known about the walls. And we have known the walls are clear as water, and one day they will ripple and tremble and slide down and down and away, into the center of the earth.

And he whispers: We are in the dream because we had it. We have dreamed it and known. And so, he says, we do not have to stay here anymore. Because the dream goes on and on without us.

ABOUT THE AUTHOR

Lydia Millet is the author of two previous novels, *Omnivores* and *George Bush, Dark Prince of Love*. She lives in New York City and Tucson, Arizona.